Laurel headed into her bedroom to get the notebook. She was lost in thought, trying to make sense of all that was unfolding. It was so hard to imagine the possibility that someone who lived right here at Wolf Lake—someone who the Torvolds knew, who the Torvolds *trusted*—could be involved in something so despicable. . . .

Suddenly she stopped. Lying on the floor in front of the bunk beds was a white envelope. Written on the front in a large, almost childish scrawl, were the words, "To the blond-haired girl."

"What on *earth* . . . ?" Laurel's voice trailed off as she bent down to pick up the envelope. She held it for a few seconds, examining the peculiar handwriting. As she did, a strange, sick feeling rose up inside her. Slowly, with trembling fingers, she opened the envelope.

Inside there was a single slip of white paper. It was unusually thick, unlike any she'd ever seen before. One edge was jagged, the sharp irregular triangles a sign that it had been ripped out of some kind of book.

On it, in the same unusual handwriting that had been on the envelope, were written four simple words: *"Keep out of it!"*

By Cynthia Blair
Published by Fawcett Books:

ALASKA ADVENTURE

Cynthia Blair

FAWCETT JUNIPER • NEW YORK

A Fawcett Juniper Book
Published by Ballantine Books
Copyright © 1995 by Cynthia Blair

Library of Congress Catalog Card Number: 95-90428

ISBN 0-449-70439-4

Manufactured in the United States of America

First Edition: November 1995

10 9 8 7 6 5 4 3 2

To Jesse

prologue

The winter snows were finally melting. Once again, fields of grass and colorful wildflowers were free to grow. The trees in the endless spruce forests sprouted another year's growth of tender needles, light green speckled with sunlight. A thick cover of vines crept across the forest floor. This was how the world had once been: untouched, untamed, perfect.

A large bear trundled across the forest, his heavy paws leaving deep prints in the soft ground. He was headed for the stream, knowing he'd find salmon in the clear, cold water.

The air was still. The silence that hung over the earth was broken only by the chirping of birds, the rustle of leaves, the occasional snap of a twig as a squirrel skittered across the forest floor.

Suddenly, the silence was broken by the sounds of engines. The bear looked up. The sight of a plane in the sky set off an automatic reaction of fear. He began to run, tearing through the forest, his large, clumsy form moving with surprising ease.

Yet he couldn't get away from the relentless whirring of the engines. The plane zeroed in on him. Closer and closer it came. Still the bear ran, terrified by the noise, terrified by the hulking form looming above. Rather than running to safety, to the sanctuary of a cave, he ran out into an open field.

From out of nowhere, a second plane appeared. The bear ran even faster, letting out a bellow that cut through the silence of the forest.

And then the loud noise of a gunshot rang through his ears. Pain ripped through his side.

Then, a second shot. The bear fell to the ground.

The last thing he saw before closing his eyes forever was a silver plane hovering overhead. And just inside the window, a flash of bright red as the gunman withdrew his arm, a satisfied smile on his face.

chapter
one

"Of course the Andersons' champagne brunch was the *loveliest* event of the season. . . . Lydia, do have some more stuffed mushrooms. They're Carter's absolute favorite, so I made sure the caterer included them in today's menu. . . ."

Laurel Adams leaned out her bedroom window, her face twisting into a disapproving grimace as her mother's voice drifted up to the second floor. An elegant garden party, a birthday celebration in her father's honor, was underway on the back lawn of her parents' stately home. And from what she could see, her mother, Catherine, had gone all out, doing her best to outshine every other hostess in the well-to-do suburbs that surrounded Washington, D.C.

From where Laurel stood, the party looked annoyingly opulent. Strings of twinkling white lights had been draped over the patio, their effect all but wasted given the fact that the late-afternoon sun was still shining brightly in the clear blue sky. The members of a five-piece chamber music group huddled in one corner of the expansive yard, struggling to make the delicate strains of their music heard over the clinking of glasses and the din of voices.

Along the edge of the patio, long narrow tables covered in crisp white linen had been set up. On them were huge platters of food, elaborate concoctions of the richest ingredients imaginable. Waiters in uniforms kept their heads bowed as they moved through the crowd, offering appetizers carefully arranged on silver trays.

With a loud bang, Laurel slammed the window shut. Flopping down on her bed, she picked up the book she'd been trying to read all afternoon, Charles Darwin's *On the Origin of Species*. But as she opened it to the page where she'd left off, she knew she'd have trouble concentrating. True, the famous book describing the great scientist's theory of evolution was something she'd wanted to dig into for the longest time. All through her freshman year at Mountainville University, her favorite professor had raved about it. Dr. Ames had insisted that her favorite pupil spend at least part of her spring break reading it, telling Laurel that after she did, she would never see the world in quite the same way again.

Even with the window shut, Laurel couldn't close out the sounds of the garden party down below. Yet she forced herself to focus on the page in front of her. Before long she got lost in her book.

A knock at the bedroom door a few minutes later startled her.

"Come in," she called. Guiltily she hid her book under the pink ruffled throw pillow that decorated her bed.

"*There* you are, Laurel." Catherine Adams stood in the doorway, her face tense. "Everyone's been asking for you. And here you are, hiding in your bedroom."

The disapproval in her mother's voice was hard to miss. Still, she saw no point in starting an argument. Laurel forced herself to smile.

"I'll be down in ten minutes." She slid off the bed, combing her hair with her fingers.

Catherine Adams studied her daughter for only a moment. "Make it five. And please, just this once, wear something appropriate."

It *is* Dad's birthday, Laurel reminded herself, gritting her teeth as she reached into the closet and pulled out a simple black dress, its price tag still dangling from the sleeve. She slipped on a pair of pumps she found stashed way in back, put on some lip gloss, and pulled back her long blond hair, fastening it with a silver clip.

It wasn't that she begrudged her parents and their friends their celebration. It was only that she wanted absolutely no part of it. As far as she was concerned, the very idea of wasting a perfectly good Sunday afternoon standing around on the velvety grass of the backyard, sipping punch and gobbling down cholesterol-filled foods with pretentious French names, was enough to make her shudder. Even worse than idling away most of a day, however, was the company.

Ever since she'd been a little girl, Laurel had felt out of place among her parents' friends. Even their children, her classmates at the finest private schools, sometimes seemed like creatures from another planet. While they could easily get excited about some silly dance or dinner party, Laurel's concept of the perfect Saturday night was camping out. Instead of strolling through the local mall, she preferred long hikes in the woods, stopping every few feet to examine an unusual plant or observe a rare species of bird. Her schoolmates' ceaseless chatter about who was going out with whom and who was switching from this prep school to that boarding school bored her to tears.

All through high school Laurel had resisted their attempts at luring her to social events—just as she'd rejected the advances of the handsome young men with perfect smiles and easy laughs who were so eager to take her out, finding them shallow and uninteresting. Because she was pretty, with her long golden blond hair, intense green eyes, and willowy frame, they never gave up trying. But because she was who she was, she never stopped trying to find ways to avoid them.

She'd also done her best to avoid her parents' parties. Checking her reflection in the mirror hanging above her dresser, Laurel frowned. She could remember dozens of parties just like this one. Even when she was little, she'd put in a brief appearance, then sneak away, trying her best not to get her fancy clothes dirty as she collected interesting rocks or chased after frogs and butterflies.

Now that she'd started at Mountainville, she'd hoped to be freed of such tedious social obligations. But spring break meant spending a full week with her parents. And while being back at home was supposed to be restful, she and her mother had picked up their ongoing conflict right where they'd left off over winter vacation. The problem was that Catherine Adams expected her daughter to spend her nine-day vacation from college shopping and visiting the girls she'd gone to high school with. Laurel, meanwhile, was determined to use all that luxurious time to organize data for her biology research project.

Being chosen to be part of a research team was an honor rarely bestowed on a member of the freshman class. Tugging on the neckline of her dress, pulling it up as high as she could, Laurel couldn't resist smiling. She'd been a star in both biology and geology during her first semester, impressing both of her science professors with her knowledge, her skill, and her dedication. Being the only freshman chosen to be part of Dr. Ames's study had been quite a feather in her cap.

Of course, her parents were baffled about why a

"young lady" like Laurel would waste her precious college years hiding out in a lab. They simply couldn't understand how important science—and becoming a scientist—was to her.

Glancing around, Laurel realized her bedroom was symbolic of the ongoing conflict between her parents and her, the perfect illustration of what *she* wanted compared to what *they* wanted. The walls were painted a delicate shade of pink that Laurel had always hated. Since she was nine years old, she'd done her best to cover them up, tacking up posters of wildlife everywhere: regal tigers poised to attack, turtles with oddly thoughtful expressions, monkeys engaged in antics that made them look amazingly human. On the white French-provincial dresser with ornate gold trim— definitely her mother's taste—was her collection of fossil sharks' teeth and whale bones.

Through her open closet door, she could see that even the clothes hanging there reflected the struggle she and her parents were engaged in. On one side hung the clothes her mother had chosen for her, designer outfits that ranged from frilly to sophisticated, all of them practically brand-new. On the other side were the oversize flannel shirts she favored, invariably wearing them over tattered jeans and a T-shirt. On the floor, a pair of high heels she hadn't worn once teetered next to a pair of dilapidated hiking boots.

Laurel sighed. She was constantly frustrated by her mother's attempts to make her over into someone she wasn't. Just thinking about what her reaction was bound to be once Laurel got up the nerve to mention her plans for the coming summer caused a knot to form in her stomach.

She'd first found out about Dr. Wells's summer research project in Alaska completely by accident.

"I have to stop at the Student Center," her best friend, Cassie Davis, had said casually after lunch one Friday a few weeks earlier. "I know it's only March, but it's time to start thinking about a summer job. Walk me over, Laurel. It'll only take a few minutes."

While Cassie ducked into the office to fill out some forms, Laurel waited in the hallway. She happened to be standing in front of the Summer Jobs bulletin board. Having nothing else to do, she ran her eyes over the index cards and slips of paper stuck up with colored pushpins. And then one of the small signs caught her eye. Her heart began to pound wildly as she read it over and over.

SUMMER RESEARCH PROJECT

ECOLOGIST SEEKS FIVE STUDENTS
to spend six weeks in Alaska
studying plants and animals

Underneath, in smaller letters, was printed "Low pay . . . but adventure guaranteed! Contact Dr. Ethan Wells, Department of Biology, Life Sciences Building, Room 8."

Laurel was still staring at the card when Cassie dashed out of the Job Placement Office. "Sorry I took so long," she said breathlessly. "First they weren't sure which form I was supposed to fill out, then they couldn't find it—"

"Cassie, look at this." Impatiently Laurel pushed her straight blond bangs out of her eyes.

"What is it?" Cassie blinked, frowning as she leaned forward and peered at the bulletin board. "I didn't know you were looking for a summer job."

"I wasn't. Until now. I mean, I figured that when I

went home to Alexandria at the end of May, I'd get the same old job I've had for the last two summers, working at that awful china shop my mother's friend owns. But this is such an incredible opportunity!"

Cassie focused on the card Laurel had pointed at. " 'Ecologist seeks five students'—*Alaska*? You're kidding, right?"

"I've never been more serious in my life." Already Laurel was scribbling the room number of Dr. Wells's office on the front cover of her spiral notebook.

As the two girls hurried to their two o'clock English Lit class, Laurel found it difficult to concentrate on Cassie's chatter. She was too busy imagining what Alaska must be like. She pictured glassy lakes surrounded by lush forests, magnificent mountain ranges with craggy peaks jutting up against the horizon, spectacular glaciers with ice blue surfaces that glowed. Going someplace so dramatic, so unspoiled, had always been a dream of hers. Going there as part of a scientific research team was almost too wonderful to imagine.

Yet that very opportunity was suddenly within her reach. If only she played her cards right. . . .

Laurel took one final peek in the mirror. After concluding that even her mother wouldn't be able to find anything to disapprove of, she headed downstairs.

"Laurel! We've all been wondering where on earth you'd disappeared to," cooed one of her parents' long-time friends, grabbing her hand the moment she stepped onto the back lawn. She was the mother of a girl with whom Laurel had graduated from high school. "Abigail's been asking about you. You must stop by to see her engagement ring. It's simply beautiful. Did she tell you that her fiancé is starting medical school in the fall?"

"Laurel, you look lovely," commented another

woman, standing a few feet behind Abigail's mother.
"Did you know Thad's home from Harvard this week?
He's been wondering whether to give you a call. Should
I tell him you're free?"

Laurel's mouth was already sore from forcing a smile
by the time she reached the punch bowl. Gratefully she
accepted a crystal glass from a waiter. She stood at the
edge of the lawn, watching the others, counting the seconds until she could escape to her bedroom—and her
book.

It quickly became clear she wouldn't be getting off as
easily as she'd hoped. Her mother had spotted her. She
was heading across the lawn in her direction with a
friend in tow.

"William insisted on saying hello," Catherine Adams
cooed, taking her daughter's hand. "He was just com-
menting on what a lovely young lady you've turned
into."

"Still chasing lizards?" William Turner, the husband
of one of her mother's close friends, greeted Laurel
with a warm smile. He'd always stood out from the
rest, more interested in what she was doing than any of
the others.

"As a matter of fact, I am."

"I'm not surprised. Rumor has it you're now a biology major at Mountainville."

"That's right."

"I also hear you're doing a crackerjack job."

She was about to tell Mr. Turner about Dr. Ames's
research project and what an honor it was to have been
chosen to work on it. But her mother caught her eye
and gave her a warning glance. Laurel knew what she
was thinking: that Mr. Turner was simply being polite
and that she'd be much better off talking less about

herself—especially her passion for science—and more about some topic of general interest.

"I'm doing my best," she said simply.

"Laurel," her mother said, "Elena North is right over there. This might be a good time to firm up your plans for working in her shop again this summer—"

William Turner raised his eyebrows. "Working in a store? Is that what you've got lined up for summer?"

Laurel took a deep breath, closing her eyes for a moment before focusing her attention on Mr. Turner. "Actually," she said boldly, "I'm spending the summer in Alaska."

"Alaska!" His eyes lit up. "How exciting!"

Laurel glanced over at her mother. Just as she'd expected, her mouth was drawn into a straight line. "What on earth are you talking about, Laurel? Such silliness!"

"It's true, Mother. Everything's all set."

"You can't be serious."

"It sounds to me as if your daughter's dead serious," William Turner commented. He nodded at Laurel encouragingly. "What's going on up there? Some research project?"

"Exactly." She made a point of keeping her eyes fixed on him as she went on, avoiding her mother's cold stare. "There's a professor at Mountainville named Ethan Wells. I talked to him a few weeks ago after I found out he was looking for some students to take with him over the summer. He's doing what's called a biological inventory of a lake, finding out what plants and animals live in and around it—"

"Laurel," her mother interrupted impatiently, "this whole thing is completely ridic—"

"That's what happens, Catherine," Mr. Turner interrupted, his tone jovial. "These kids of ours grow up. One minute we're forcing strained bananas down their throats, and the next thing we know they're off on their own, making their own decisions, planning their own lives. . . ."

Laurel cast him a grateful look. Yet her mother didn't appear to be convinced.

"Laurel, this is certainly something your father and I are going to discuss. Your plans for this summer are anything but definite. Why, up until this moment, I simply assumed you'd be living at home, socializing with your friends, and going back to Elena's shop."

"Mother, everything's already in place. I've arranged it all with Dr. Wells—"

"That's enough for now, Laurel." Her mother's tone made it clear the subject was closed. "Come along with me. The Prestons have been asking about you for weeks. They're anxious to hear all about your first year of college."

"Good luck, kid," Mr. Turner whispered with a wink.

Laurel didn't have a chance to reply before her mother dragged her away.

"How *could* you?" Mrs. Adams cried. She turned her back on Laurel, gazing out at the back lawn through the huge bay window that nearly covered an entire wall of the study. "Embarrassing me like that in front of my friends!"

"I didn't mean to embarrass you, Mother," Laurel insisted, struggling to remain calm. "I was simply telling you and Mr. Turner my plans for the summer."

"I think what your mother means," Laurel's father, Carter, interjected, "is that she would have preferred that you clear your summer plans with her first."

"It's more than that." Catherine turned around, her arms folded firmly across her chest. Behind her, Laurel could see the caterer's crew cleaning up, folding tablecloths, and carrying huge floral centerpieces back to their trucks. "I can't believe you actually thought your father and I would give you permission to go traipsing off to ... to *Alaska*, of all places. ..."

She let her voice trail off, meanwhile staring at her daughter coldly. "What were you thinking? Or maybe you weren't thinking at all. Maybe this is simply some act of teenage rebelliousness."

Laurel stood very still, resisting the urge to yell or beg or run from the room. Instead, she looked her mother squarely in the eye. "Surely you must understand how important this is to me."

For the first time, her mother's gaze wavered. As Catherine Adams glanced at her husband, Laurel felt a surge of strength rise up inside.

"I've wanted to be a biologist ever since I was a little girl," she went on, sounding more and more sure of herself. "You know how much I've always loved being outdoors, collecting things, studying nature. But I've always done it on my own. Everything I know, I've taught myself or learned from books. I've never had a chance to do any fieldwork, to get out there and really do what research biologists do. You said yourself you couldn't understand how I could bear to spend so much time cooped up in a lab."

"What your mother meant," Carter Adams said, "is that a girl your age should be out having fun. Going to parties, meeting people—"

"That may be fine for other girls my age, but it's not what I want." Laurel looked at her father pleadingly. "Don't you know me well enough to see that?"

"But Alaska!" her mother cried. "It's so far away. So wild. So ... so cold."

"It's not cold in the summer, Mother. Dr. Wells told me all about it. The area we're going to, the Kenai Peninsula, is southwest of Anchorage, in the lower part of the state. The only snow I'm likely to encounter is at high elevations, up near the tops of mountains. The lake where we'll be doing our research is moderate, not too hot and certainly not cold—"

"You're talking about this as if you've already decided you're going," Carter commented.

"I am," Laurel said, her voice soft but firm. "This is a once-in-a-lifetime opportunity. I can't pass it up. No one, not even you, can ask me to."

This time the look her parents exchanged was one of resignation.

"It sounds as if her mind's made up, Catherine."

"I suppose Will Turner was right. Children reach a certain age and suddenly you can't control them anymore." Pointedly she added, "Even when you see they're making rash decisions, there's nothing you can do but stand by and watch, hoping they learn from their mistakes."

Ordinarily, words like those would have hit Laurel like a blow. But inwardly she was rejoicing. Her parents were going to let her go! Maybe they weren't being as supportive as she would have liked, but at least they weren't standing in her way. And that meant that the fantasy she'd harbored for so long was about to become reality.

chapter
two

"Guess what, Cassie! I'm going! I'm really going!"

Laurel's squeal was so enthusiastic and so loud that Cassie Davis held the receiver away from her ear.

"Going *where*?" she finally asked.

"Alaska, that's where!"

Cassie kicked off her sneakers and stretched across the brown leather couch that lined one wall of the den. She'd made a point of taking Laurel's long-distance call in this room, the most comfortable in the Davis's tumbledown Victorian house on the edge of Mountainville, Vermont. It had originally been a sun room. Now, the French doors that opened onto the garden were the only reminder that this had at one time been a place of leisure.

The walls were covered in floor-to-ceiling bookshelves, stacked with the thick volumes her father used to teach anthropology at the university. He graded his students' work at the huge mahogany desk in the center of the room—a desk piled so high with books and notes and papers that the haphazard stacks threatened to slide off at any moment. The dark red Persian rug with its intricate design and thick pile gave the room a hushed, somber feeling, as if this were a place for thinking deep thoughts.

"I gather you're talking about that nature trip with Dr. what's-his-name," said Cassie.

"Dr. Wells," Laurel corrected her. "Dr. Ethan Wells. And not only am I still thinking about it, my bags are practically packed!"

"So good old Mom and Dad finally agreed."

Laurel laughed. "They nearly had a fit. You should have seen the look on my mother's face when I told her I intended to spend the summer in *Alaska*, of all places. I get the feeling my parents haven't figured out yet that it's part of the United States."

Cassie was barely listening as Laurel chattered away about her adventurous summer ahead. She was too busy studying the print hanging on the wall of her father's study. Distractedly she twirled a strand of short, curly red hair around one finger. She'd seen that etching a thousand times before but had never given it much thought. Now, her mind began to wander as she dissected the techniques used by the artist who'd created it: the composition, the colors, the way dark and light were used in contrast. . . .

She'd only been on spring break for two days, yet she'd already put all thoughts of her academic subjects on a back burner. Friday afternoon, right after her last class, she headed across campus, toward home. Without even stopping for a snack, she'd gone up to her room, taken out her tubes of acrylics, and begun a new painting.

What bliss it was, knowing she had a full nine days to devote to her one true love: her artwork. Almost immediately she forgot about catching up on the reading for her English Literature class. She'd also forgotten all her intentions of boning up on calculus, trying to make sense of symbols that since September had seemed like little more than squiggles to her. There would be time for that—later. For now, she was going to indulge herself. Every morning, after breakfast, she would open her paints and lose herself in the exhilarating act of *creating*.

She'd wanted to take an art course or two, just as she had all through high school. But months earlier, when she was putting together her schedule for her freshman year at Mountainville University, her parents stood firm.

"It's time for you to get serious, Cassie," her father, Professor Lawrence Davis, had insisted. She'd cringed when he waved his hand through the air dismissively, acting as if the paints spread out on the dining-room table were nothing more than toys. "I expect you to take a full academic load this year. You're in college now. You've got to start thinking about your future, deciding what field you want to go into. I recommend you take courses in as many different areas as you can manage. Math, science, the humanities. . . ."

"Your father's right." As usual, her mother, also a professor at the university, had been in complete agreement with him. "You're turning out to be a bit of a late bloomer, Cassie. Not that there's anything wrong with that. It's just that you have yet to find yourself. If you'd like, I can ask around and find out which classes would be the most worthwhile for you to take. . . ."

Her freshman year wasn't even over yet, and Cassie had already considered half a dozen majors. Her first-semester archaeology course had gotten her fired up for a good two weeks. When that faded, she got excited about economics . . . for the better part of a week. Art history had her eating, sleeping, and breathing French Impressionists and German Expressionists for close to a month.

Yet in the end, none of them stuck. She always retreated home or to the university's art studio to paint. For her, art was more than a hobby. It was a passion.

In a way, she envied her best friend. Laurel was only a freshman, but already she had no doubts about what direction she wanted her studies and her life to follow. In fact, Cassie's parents had mentioned her best friend more than once, citing her as an example of a "young woman who had her head screwed on straight."

Cassie suspected they understood Laurel Adams better than they understood their own daughter. After all, Laurel, like them, was passionate about her work. For that matter, even Cassie's fifteen-year-old brother, Mark, was a source of that same kind of irritation. He'd been a math whiz his entire life, and there was no doubt in anyone's mind that he'd stick with what he excelled at.

It had been Cassie's idea to live at home during her college years, earning her degree right here in her hometown. Growing up, she'd found being part of a college community fascinating. She'd always been proud that her parents worked at the university that was the center of the small New England town.

Yet having two parents who were professors at the same school where she was a student was turning out to be confining. They had something to say about everything she did: not only which courses she took and which professors she chose, but even which gym classes she signed up for. At night, around the dinner table, Lawrence and Virginia Davis engaged in endless discussion of the goings-on at Mountainville.

"Cassie?" Laurel was suddenly saying, her voice impatient. "Are you listening?"

"Sorry, Laurel. I guess I let my mind wander." Cassie made a point of focusing on the telephone conversation. "Well, spending the summer in Alaska may not be my cup of tea, but I'm glad you're going. Just make sure the bears don't get you!"

"Frankly, I'm much more worried about the mosquitoes," Laurel returned, laughing.

Cassie felt guilty for having been caught daydreaming. Her best friend simply knew her too well. She couldn't help letting her mind drift off at the oddest times—when she was in class, for example, or even when, like now, she was on the phone with someone calling from hundreds of miles away.

Her two main passions, art and daydreaming, had something in common. And that was that they both took her out of her everyday life. In part, preferring to live in a world of fantasy was simply her nature. Yet there was another important factor that contributed to her tendency to retreat into herself: the fact that she'd always been chubby.

She wasn't exactly what anyone would call fat, but she'd always been plump enough that the other kids used to tease her about her weight. The fact that she was also uncoordinated didn't help. She was the type who was always picked last to be on a team, the girl who elicited groans from the others whenever it was her turn to bat during a baseball game.

Now, whenever she looked into the mirror, she had to admit she wasn't that different from a lot of the other girls. During high school, she'd shot up a few inches, her curves changing enough to give her a silhouette that was pleasantly round, even if it was a little too full. Her coloring was striking, and she told herself that people were more likely to notice her full head of curly red hair and her bright blue eyes than the extra ten pounds she carried. Yet she still felt different. Between her natural tendency to be shy and her self-consciousness over being plump, she preferred being alone, pursuing what was important to her. When Saturday night rolled around, she was happy staying home by herself or with a friend, watching TV or renting a video—usually topping off the evening by ordering in a pizza or whipping up a batch of brownies.

"Well, Laurel," Cassie said, determined to stop letting her mind wander and instead concentrate on the phone conversation, "it sounds like you've got a great summer ahead of you."

"I'm already counting the days!" Laurel assured her. "How about you? Have you thought about what you're going to do?"

"I'm looking forward to spending three long months at home. Just think—no classes, no grades, and no exams. Oh, I'm still hoping to find a job somewhere in town. But mostly I want to paint. I've got a million ideas that I simply haven't had the time to follow up on, thanks to that weekly paper in English Lit and those problem sets in Calculus and everything else that's been keeping me too busy to breathe all semester."

The girls had just hung up when Cassie's father poked his head in the doorway.

"Sorry. I didn't realize you were in here."

"That's okay. I've finished talking on the phone."

"I wanted to get a book."

"Help yourself. We've got thousands."

Dr. Davis scanned the shelves, his head bent to one side as he read the titles on the books' spines.

"Who called?" he asked pleasantly.

"Laurel."

"How is she? Is she enjoying spring break?"

"She's so focused on her summer that she's barely thinking about spring." Dragging herself off the couch and perching on the thickly padded arm, Cassie continued, "Laurel's got this crazy plan. Believe it or not, she's going to Alaska this summer."

"Really?" Dr. Davis sat down at his desk, putting the book he'd retrieved from the shelf off to one side. He fixed his gaze on Cassie, pressing the tips of his fingers together to form an inverted V.

"There's some research project one of the professors at the university is running. I think he's a biologist."

"Actually, he's an ecologist."

It took a moment for the meaning of her father's words to register. "You mean you've heard about this project?"

"Certainly. Ethan Wells and I have been friends for years. We met when we both served on the university's undergraduate admissions committee." He paused for a moment before adding, "As a matter of fact, he called me just last week."

"Really?" Cassie was barely listening. She was much less interested in hearing about her father's friends at the university than she was in studying the outline of his silhouette, wondering how she could capture on canvas the odd shadows cast by the late-afternoon light.

"It was you he wanted to talk about."

"Me?" Cassie's interest was suddenly piqued. "Why on earth would some science professor I've never even met want to talk to me?"

"He remembered a conversation he and I had about you last spring. It was back when you were trying to decide whether to go away to college or to stay right here in Mountainville."

Cassie squirmed uncomfortably.

"Ethan told me he remembered my saying I was concerned about your reluctance to try new things," Lawrence Davis went on.

"Daddy," Cassie protested, feeling her cheeks redden,

"do you have to go around telling our personal business to total strangers?"

"Ethan's not a stranger," Dr. Davis said gently. "He's a friend."

Cassie was growing more and more uneasy. She wasn't sure where all this was leading . . . but the gnawing feeling in her stomach told her there was an excellent chance it would turn out to be a place she wouldn't be pleased about.

"Go on," she urged, swallowing hard.

"I'll cut to the chase. Cassie, Dr. Wells wants you to be part of his research team this summer."

It was Cassie who finally broke the long, heavy silence that followed Professor Davis's announcement.

"You're joking, right? You're just trying to scare me into taking school more seriously. Or . . . or maybe into thinking about transferring to another college. Or—"

"I'm not joking, Cassie. This is a wonderful opportunity. Your mother and I have made a mistake in babying you. Of course, we love having you here all the time, but in the long run we're not doing you much of a service. You've never been off on your own, learning to take care of yourself. It's high time you spread your wings a little. And this is the perfect way."

"But—but I don't know anything about biology!" Cassie's mind raced as she struggled to come up with a convincing argument why this plan of her father's was absurd. "And Alaska's so far away. And—and—"

"Ethan and I discussed all that. He understands that you're not a budding scientist. He's willing to teach you whatever you need to know. What's even more valuable to him are your other traits. He knows you're conscientious and responsible and hardworking. . . ."

For the second time in the past few minutes, Cassie stopped listening. She was off in another world. But this time, it wasn't one of colors and shapes. It was one of mosquitoes and bears, wet feet and aching muscles. She pictured herself in an untamed wilderness, thousands of miles away from home. She saw a girl who was tired, lonely, uncomfortable, and more than a little scared.

She was tempted to protest, to rack her brain until she came up with a way of getting her father to change his mind. But the determination in his voice told her it was no use. And if she knew anything at all about her mother, she could be certain she felt exactly the same way.

The decision had been made . . . and there was no going back. Like it or not, she was going to Alaska. Somehow, even knowing that her best friend was going with her wasn't enough to keep a hard knot from forming in the pit of her stomach—a knot Cassie suspected wouldn't go away until after she'd come back home to Mountainville at the end of the summer.

chapter
three

"Dr. Ethan Wells. Department of Biology."

Mariah Burke read the words on the plaque aloud, her voice dripping with disdain even though there was no one around to hear. In fact, as she stood outside the door at the end of an undistinguished pale gray cinder-block hallway in the deserted basement of the Life Sciences building, her books balanced casually on one hip, she could have been the only creature in the world.

The only *living* creature, at least. Lining the corridor were large glass cases displaying endless varieties of insects, butterflies, and reptiles—all of them dead. Mariah had barely given them a glance as she'd come down the hall, her reluctance about this mission reflected in the slowness of her pace.

Yes, this was the place. She hesitated a moment longer. Then, letting out a sigh, she rapped on the door.

"Come in," answered a deep voice from within.

Here goes, thought Mariah. She paused for a moment, smoothing her long black hair, hanging down her back in thick waves. Then she threw open the door and strode inside.

Her first impression was that she'd stepped into an enclave of complete chaos. The metal shelving that lined two of the walls was covered with cheerful clutter, not only books and journals and stacks of papers, but

24

also rocks, fossils, and the types of specimens she'd breezed past in the display cases. The large metal desk was similarly covered with disheveled piles of books and papers. A computer was pushed off to one side.

Hanging over the desk, next to a bulletin board covered with photographs, newspaper articles, and Post-its with telephone numbers scrawled across them, was a large poster. On it was a photograph of a magnificent mountain range. Jagged black rock reached high into the sky, the pure white of the snow-covered peaks a startling contrast. Underneath, in bold letters, were the words "Alaska: The Last Frontier."

"Dr. Wells?" asked Mariah.

"That's me."

He sat at his desk, a stack of papers laid out before him. He was younger than she'd expected, probably in his thirties. Through wire-rimmed glasses peered a pair of piercing dark eyes. Thick, wavy black hair covered his head, curling just over his collar. He was dressed casually in a plaid flannel shirt, well-worn jeans, and a pair of scuffed brown leather boots.

"I'm Mariah Burke. Dr. Lewis suggested I talk to you."

"Ah, yes. I've been expecting you."

"You have?"

"Nate Lewis called me this morning. Take a seat."

Mariah was suddenly uneasy. She could feel her confidence slipping away. She hadn't expected Dr. Lewis, her genetics professor, to call ahead.

He was the one who'd first told Mariah about Dr. Wells's research project. Mariah was the star pupil in his class. The fact that she was also the only freshman in a class full of sophomores and juniors made her straight-A average even more outstanding.

When Dr. Lewis had called Mariah into his office, she couldn't imagine what he wanted to say.

"Mariah," Dr. Lewis began, taking off the thick glasses that he always wore during class, "I think you have an exciting future ahead of you. You are an excellent scientist. You quickly grasp even the most difficult concepts, your lab work is impeccable. . . ."

Mariah was about to say "Thank you" when Dr. Lewis shook his head.

"But there is something missing. You have no experience with the practical side of science. Everything you know, you've learned from books. There's so much more to the natural world than what you can read about on the printed page."

Before she could defend herself, pointing out that a pre-med student majoring in biology had little need for anything other than book knowledge, Dr. Lewis handed her a Xerox copy of a journal article. "Have you met Dr. Wells?" he asked.

Mariah shook her head.

"Ah. That's too bad. Ethan Wells is someone you should know."

She glanced at the title of the article, still not understanding. " 'Limnology of Three Small Lakes on the Kenai Peninsula, Alaska,' " she read aloud. With a shrug, she told him, "I'm afraid I don't understand."

"Limnology is the study of freshwater lakes and ponds. It's just one of Dr. Wells's interests, and one of the many areas he's incorporating into the research project he's conducting in the field this summer. He's taking a group of students with him to Alaska. He's running a project that involves really getting out there. Actually *experiencing* the world of science, Mariah, rather than simply observing it from afar. Being part of something like that is as different from studying science in a lab as ... as the difference between reading about Egypt and getting on a camel and traveling through the desert to the Great Pyramid."

Smiling, Dr. Lewis added, "I think you would benefit greatly from an experience like this."

Mariah's first reaction had been one of horror. The idea of spending two months slogging around Alaska in a pair of hip boots, brandishing a spray can of insect repellent, was anything but appealing. But slowly it occurred to her that Dr. Lewis wasn't really giving her much of a choice. He was Mountainville University's pre-med advisor, advising undergraduate students who hoped to get into medical school one day, and she'd been hoping that he'd write her a glowing recommendation when it was time to apply.

Then there was the issue of finding a way of making med schools sit up and take notice. A project like this might be just the thing she needed in a couple of years to distinguish her from the hundreds of other applicants to the most prestigious, competitive medical schools.

Besides, she reasoned, if she went ahead and applied, and then wasn't accepted as a member of Dr. Wells's research team, at least she'd be able to go back to Dr. Lewis and tell him she'd tried. Then he'd keep her in mind when something more to her liking came along ... something she could do *indoors*, far away from mud and bugs and long days of strenuous effort.

"Tell me a little about yourself," Dr. Wells said congenially, folding his hands on the desk in front of him. "Where are you from?"

"Beverly Hills." Automatically Mariah stuck her chin up a littler higher. It was a defiant gesture she'd picked up since coming to school back east. Whenever people heard she was from one of the wealthiest sections of Los Angeles, they either teased her or, even worse, silently made their own assumptions. "My father, Oliver Burke, is a staff surgeon at the UCLA Biomedical Center."

"He's a plastic surgeon, isn't he?"

Mariah's chin rose even higher. "Plastic surgery isn't all nose jobs and tummy tucks, you know. He's done groundbreaking work in the area of developing new techniques for grafting skin on burn victims—"

"I know all about Dr. Oliver Burke's revolutionary research," Dr. Wells interrupted, nodding. "He's come up with some impressive results. Is your mother in the medical field, as well?"

"My mother died when I was ten," Mariah said brusquely. As always, talking about anything the least bit personal made her fidgety. The idea of people knowing more about her than they had to made her feel vulnerable. In her eyes, it gave them an advantage.

Even before Dr. Wells had a chance to react, she continued, "I have two older brothers who are following in my father's footsteps. Peter's in his second year of medical school at Columbia University and Todd is a resident at Peter Bent Brigham Hospital in Boston."

"And you, Mariah? Is that the direction in which you're headed, as well?"

"I plan to go to medical school."

What she didn't add was, "If I get in." She did think it, however. In fact, she thought about the uncertainty of her future all the time. Her father simply assumed she'd follow in his footsteps. As for her brothers, they'd been teasing her about how much better they were at just about everything ever since she was a little girl. In fact, Mariah was driven more by her determination to show her two big brothers she was every bit as good as they were than by wanting to impress her father. She was desperate to prove she was just as smart as they were, just as accomplished. . . .

In fact, when her boyfriend, Kurt, had chosen to stay in California and attend college at UCLA, she'd actually been a little relieved. This way, she reasoned, she'd be able to fly home to see him during school vacations, but she'd be free to concentrate on her studies during the year.

"If it's med school you're heading for," Dr. Wells was saying, "I'm not quite sure why this project of mine is of interest to you."

Mariah's heart began pounding. She didn't want to admit she wanted something outstanding to add to her record, something to impress not only Dr. Lewis but also the admissions directors at medical schools like Harvard and Columbia. She didn't dare say that a summer doing research in Alaska was just the thing to make her applications stand out. So she took a deep breath before answering, measuring her words carefully.

"What I want most is to become a doctor. But I believe that in order to understand the human body, it's crucial to understand the whole natural world. We are, after all, just one small part of it, another piece in a huge, complex puzzle."

"I see." Dr. Wells was silent for a long time, staring at the stacks of papers and books piled up haphazardly on his desk. "Well, Mariah, I've already decided to include you in the project."

Mariah's mouth dropped open. But before she had a chance to decide whether she was glad or disappointed, she heard someone else come into the room behind her. Glancing over her shoulder, she saw a tall, muscular young man leaning in the doorway of Dr. Wells's office. He was quite good-looking, with even features, a thick head of curly dark blond hair, and striking blue eyes.

He wore ripped jeans and a snug-fitting Mountainville University Athletic Department T-shirt. But what struck Mariah most was his arrogant demeanor.

"Hope I'm not interrupting anything," he said, looking Mariah up and down.

For the first time since she'd come in, she felt self-conscious. Her expensive designer outfit suddenly seemed out of place here, a peculiar contrast to the jeans and casual shirts both he and Dr. Wells were wearing. In a nervous gesture, she pushed the row of solid gold bangle bracelets she was wearing up her arm.

Casting him the coldest look she could manage, Mariah said, "Dr. Wells and I are discussing this summer's research project in Alaska."

"Oh, yeah? What, are you covering this for the school paper or something?"

"Mariah's a biology major, too," said Dr. Wells.

Trip laughed. "A regular Madame Curie, huh?"

She could feel her cheeks turning red—not from embarrassment, but from anger. The last thing she was in the mood for was some cocky science jock putting down women in science, falling back on the cliché of comparing her to the best-known female scientist of all time.

"Marie Curie was a physicist, not a biologist," she said sharply. "I thought everyone knew that."

Dr. Wells cut in with, "I guess you two haven't met before, so I'll make this a formal introduction. Mariah Burke, this is Trip Raynor. Trip, Mariah. Trip's a sophomore, Mariah's a freshman. . . ." Dr. Wells shrugged. "Anything else you need to know, just ask."

Mariah hesitated before reaching out her hand to shake. Trip responded by folding his arms across his chest, peering down at her through his brilliant blue eyes. "How're you doing, Mariah?"

"Trip?" she repeated. "What kind of name is that?"

"A nickname. My real name is Charles Edward Raynor ... the Third." He shrugged. "Ever since I was a kid growing up in New York City, everybody forgot about the first three names ... and concentrated on the fact that I was 'the Third.' "

"Oh, I get it," Mariah observed dryly. "Triple."

"Bright girl," Trip said to Dr. Wells.

"That's enough, Trip," the professor cut in.

Mariah was tempted to launch into a tirade on exactly what she thought of arrogant young men like him who built themselves up by putting other people down— especially women. But she remained silent, not wanting to leave Dr. Wells with a bad impression.

Instead, she said curtly, "Dr. Wells and I will be finished soon."

"Hey, if you two are talking about the trip to Alaska, count me in." Trip had come into the office, sitting down on the edge of the metal desk.

Slowly the meaning of his words sank in. "Don't tell me you're—"

"Grizzlies and black flies, here I come." With so much ease and confidence that someone who didn't know better might have thought this was *his* office, he planted his sneakered foot firmly in the middle of a vacant swivel chair.

Mariah looked at Dr. Wells pleadingly. Perhaps she'd simply misunderstood. . . .

"That's right," the professor said. "Trip's part of the field crew."

"Sounds like it's you and me, babe," Trip said lightly. Ignoring the icy look Dr. Wells cast him, he added, "Have you made your final decision about who else is coming?"

"There'll be five of you." After spending a few seconds rummaging around the mound of books and papers on his desk, Dr. Wells retrieved a piece of paper. Referring to it, he said, "In addition to you two, I've got a freshman named Laurel Adams on board—"

"Never heard of her," Trip said loftily.

Mariah stiffened. "I have."

Not only had she heard of Laurel Adams, she'd spent the entire year secretly competing with her. When Laurel was the only freshman picked to work on Dr. Ames's research project, Mariah was furious. *That* was an honor that would have impressed even Harvard Medical School.

"The daughter of one of my colleagues here at the university is also coming along. Her name is Cassandra Davis."

Trip frowned. "I don't remember any Cassandras in any of my science courses."

"She's taking mostly liberal arts courses." In response to Mariah's raised eyebrows, he added, "But I'm confident she'll be a valuable contributor to the project."

"Who's number five?" Mariah asked, anxious to move on.

"Russell Corcoran. He's—"

"Oh, no!" Trip groaned dramatically. "Not Nature Boy!"

"Nature Boy?" Mariah repeated.

"That's our nickname for him. He's the kind of guy who's perfectly at home in the woods but has a hard time carrying on a conversation with anyone of his own species."

"It's true that Russ is sharp when it comes to science," said Dr. Wells. "He grew up on a nature preserve, where his father was the station manager."

Mariah just shrugged. "Sounds like a pretty mixed bag, if you ask me."

"We've got a good cross section," Dr. Wells agreed. "I think it's going to work out well. When we combine everyone's strengths and weaknesses, we should end up with a nicely balanced group."

"Wait a second." Trip was counting on his fingers. "We've got Russ and me . . . and three *girls*?"

Mariah could feel her blood boil. "What's wrong with that?"

"Gee, Dr. Wells, isn't that kind of unfair? I mean, going off to Alaska to do research is an incredible opportunity. Why are you wasting it on so many girls? Speaking realistically, how many of them are actually going to go ahead and become real, working scientists?"

Mariah opened her mouth, ready to launch a tirade against this Neanderthal whose ideas sounded as if they were rooted somewhere back in the nineteenth century. But before she could get the first word out, Dr. Wells interrupted, his voice soothing but firm.

"Trip," he said, "it's important that we get one thing straight, right from the start. The six of us are going up to Alaska as a *team*. We're going to be working closely together, every step of the way. That means we'll be relying on each other. Things are going to come up all the time, things none of us can anticipate. We're going to have to look out for each other—not only to make the project work, but also to make sure all of us come back home at the end of the summer, safe and sound."

Trip's reaction was a casual shrug, accompanied by the offhanded comment, "Whatever you say."

As for Mariah, at the moment she was less concerned with whether or not the research team was going to work together harmoniously than with Dr. Wells's

comment about coming back home at the end of the
summer, safe and sound. Involuntarily her eyes traveled across the room to the poster hanging above the
professor's desk.

"Alaska," it read. "The Last Frontier." Mariah swallowed hard. She only hoped that being part of this research project wouldn't turn out to be a mistake,
offering more adventure than the daughter of a promi-
nent Beverly Hills plastic surgeon could stand.

chapter
four

"Okay. Let's run through the list one more time, just to make sure we haven't forgotten anything." Dr. Wells stood outside the run-down Bio Department van. The van was parked near the loading dock of the Life Sciences building and surrounded by so many suitcases, backpacks, sleeping bags, duffel bags, coolers, and other assorted items that it was hard to believe everything would fit.

"First item: fish traps?"

"Check," called Trip, crouched inside the van.

"Coolers?"

"They're over here," Laurel replied, glancing over from where she was standing, next to a pile of gear sitting in the parking lot beside the van's open-door side.

"Scintillation vials, collecting bottles, thermometers, dip nets, Van Doren water sampler?"

"Got those, too," Trip reported.

Cassie stood on the edge of the parking lot, her hands jammed deep inside the pockets of her nylon jacket as she watched. She knew she should volunteer to help. But ever since she'd arrived ten minutes earlier, she'd stood off to one side, squinting in the early morning June sun. She told herself she was waiting for someone to tell her what to do, since she didn't want to be in the way. In truth, she was nearly paralyzed by the gnawing in the pit of her stomach. At that moment, she would have given anything to be back home in her own bed.

Her mind was reeling. It's not too late to back out, she thought. I don't care what my parents think. I don't care what Dr. Wells thinks. I can't go through with this. . . .

"Hey, Cassie!" Dr. Wells suddenly called. "How about bringing your stuff over? We'll start packing it into the van."

Glancing over in his direction, she saw that the professor was offering her a friendly smile. "Okay," she returned.

But before she had a chance to lean down and pick up her overstuffed duffel bag, a dilapidated car turned off the main road and into the parking lot, then headed over in their direction. For the moment, packing up the van was forgotten. Dr. Wells strolled over to greet whoever it was who'd arrived.

"Russ! Good to see you!"

"Hope I'm not late, Dr. Wells. Dwight had a little trouble getting his car started."

"No problem—especially since we can't leave without him." Leaning his head in through the open window, Dr. Wells added, "Thanks for volunteering to drive the van back from the airport, Dwight."

Cassie watched as Russ Corcoran, the fifth student member of the research team, climbed out of the front seat, then dragged a canvas duffel bag and a sleeping bag out of the back. She hadn't yet had a chance to form much of an impression of Russ. At the planning meeting Dr. Wells had held a few weeks earlier, there hadn't been much opportunity for the members of the project to get to know each other. They'd been too busy listening to Dr. Wells brief them on the trip ahead.

There had been so much to take in! Cassie had felt

out of place and overwhelmed as she'd watched the others scribble page after page of notes. She was still having trouble believing that she was a part of all this. Even at that meeting, she hadn't been able to take in the fact that she was really headed for six weeks in Alaska. According to what Dr. Wells was saying, she, like the others, would be roughing it in a log cabin on a lake in the middle of nowhere, collecting samples of fish and insects, looking out for different varieties of birds, scouting around for wildflowers. . . .

It was all part of the study he was doing on one of the larger lakes southwest of Anchorage, on a piece of land called the Kenai Peninsula that jutted into the Gulf of Alaska. He was trying to answer the question of why some lakes have rooted plants in them and others have plankton, a form of free-floating algae. The two were in competition, he'd told them. The weeds took the nutrients out of the lake, making it impossible for plankton to grow. The plankton, in turn, blocked the sunlight, making it impossible for plants to grow. The question Dr. Wells was trying to answer was whether or not there was any particular property of the lake that determined which won out. In order to do that, it was necessary to take a "biological inventory" of the lake, determining all forms of plant life and animal life that lived in and around it.

"All right, Cassie. Let's get those bags of yours into the van."

Dr. Wells's voice snapped her out of her daydream and back to the task at hand. She bent down to pick up her duffel bag. Letting out a loud groan, she managed to lift it mere inches off the ground.

"Need some help?" Russ had come over, his own bag slung over his shoulder. He seemed shy, his brown eyes not quite looking into hers. Nervously he pushed back the straight dark brown bangs that kept falling into his eyes.

"Oh, no, thanks. I—well, on second thought, I guess I need all the help I can get."

He'd already grabbed hold of her bag. "Wow. This is pretty heavy. What've you got in here?"

"I wasn't sure what to pack," Cassie replied apologetically. Picking up her sleeping bag, she fell into step with him as he crossed the parking lot. "Even though I crammed everything I could think of into that bag, I'm sure it'll turn out I brought all the wrong stuff."

"You're Cassie, right?" Russ smiled shyly. "I'm Russ Corcoran."

"I know. I remember your name from the planning meeting."

"I've been meaning to ask you . . . aren't your parents on the faculty at Mountainville?"

She cast him a wary look. "That's right. My father, Lawrence Davis, is in the anthropology department. My mom, Virginia Davis, is in political science."

"It must be interesting, having parents who are college professors."

"Right now, I wish they were anything *but* college professors. The fact that a million years ago my father served on some stupid admissions committee with Dr. Wells is the whole reason I'm here in the first place."

"You mean this wasn't your idea?"

Cassie shook her head. "I don't know the first thing about science. And tromping off to the wilds of Alaska is probably my last choice in the entire universe of how to spend my summer vacation." Her voice had become strained, and her eyes were suddenly shiny and wet. "If I had my choice—"

She never finished. They'd reached the van, and Dr. Wells came over to help load their bags.

"I think that just about does it," he announced. "All we're missing now is Mariah."

A few minutes passed before a lone figure appeared, leisurely rounding the corner of the Life Sciences building. The tall, thin young woman ambling toward them was wearing a brand-new pair of tight-fitting jeans, a purple suede jacket, and fashionable brown leather boots with chunky heels. Her nearly waist-length black hair surrounded her face like a veil, setting off her remarkably delicate features. Over her shoulder was slung a backpack, and in one hand she held a nylon sleeping bag. Both the pack and the sleeping bag looked brand-new, as if they'd been delivered by L. L. Bean just the day before.

"We're going to the airport in *that*?" Mariah cried by way of a greeting. Dropping her baggage onto the ground, she placed her hands on her hips. "You've *got* to be kidding."

Trip poked his head out of the van long enough to cast her a scathing look. "Glad you could make it, Mariah. I hope our early departure didn't interrupt your beauty sleep."

"I'm amazed you can be so witty before you've had your cornflakes," she shot back with an arrogant toss of her head. Her pale hazel eyes, gleaming with disdain, rested on Trip for a few seconds before she looked away.

"You're late, Mariah," Dr. Wells said firmly. "When I said I planned to leave promptly at seven, I meant it. It's already seven-twenty."

"Sorry."

"Throw your gear into the back and climb in," Dr. Wells instructed, ignoring her insolent tone. "We've got a plane to catch."

"These vans are incredibly comfortable," Laurel said

to Mariah as everyone got settled in the van. Trip, who claimed to be an expert at maneuvering the congested roads around the airport, sat in front with Dr. Wells, playing navigator. Laurel and Cassie were in the first set of backseats, with Russ and Mariah right behind. Dwight was in the back corner. "There's plenty of room for storage, too."

"I'm sure it's perfectly adequate for those people who love the great outdoors and all that," Mariah grumbled. "Personally, I'd be happy if we spent the entire six weeks living in one of those trailers that's fitted with a full bathroom, a microwave, and air-conditioning."

Cassie cast a wary look at Laurel. As the van pulled out of the university parking lot, a wave of fear came over her. As she'd suspected, even having her best friend along on this trip wasn't as comforting as she would have liked.

As if the feeling of being uprooted weren't already strong enough, Dr. Wells suddenly announced, "We're off!" in a hearty voice. If Cassie had ever believed there was a chance to back out, that chance had just passed.

"Is everybody settled in back there?" the professor asked once he'd veered onto the highway that, after a ride of an hour or so, would lead to the airport. "I'd like to take advantage of the fact that right now you're all a captive audience to remind you that what I need from you most over the next six weeks is your complete cooperation. A little team spirit wouldn't hurt, either." Glancing into the rearview mirror so that his eyes met Mariah's, he added, "That means keeping to whatever schedule I've laid out."

"Aye, aye, sir," Mariah muttered under her breath.

"But it also means everyone's willingness to pitch in, without being asked. We're going to encounter all kinds of different situations up there, many of which are new. If we work together, we'll all work better.

"Actually, I'm not that concerned about getting the group to act as a whole. As I say, I've run field trips like this before, and I've never run into any problems. I've picked each and every one of you carefully. You all have something to add, something invaluable."

Trip glanced back over his shoulder. "The three lovely ladies on our trip certainly make it more pleasurable, but what about their ability to keep up?"

Cassie felt Laurel tense up. Behind her, she heard Mariah mumble, "What a turkey." But before any of the girls had a chance to voice their protests, Dr. Wells broke in.

"Trip, one of the best ways to get this group acting as a single unit is to keep comments like that to yourself. As I've said, I put a lot of thought into everybody who's been invited to be part of the team. Every individual—and I mean every one—is bringing some real strengths to the project.

"Trip, you've already proven yourself a capable scientist in my classes and in my lab. I think you have some real leadership capabilities, as well, although I'd like to see how you function in a group before I make any definitive judgments. Laurel, you've also distinguished yourself with your lab work. Dr. Ames was very pleased with your work during second semester.

"Russ, if you don't mind, I'd like to fill the others in on your background." When Russ gave a nod of his head, Dr. Wells went on. "For those of you who haven't yet had the chance to talk to Russ, he grew up on a nature preserve in New Hampshire. If you've ever wanted to see a dyed-in-the-wool naturalist, he's your man. Mariah, your comprehension of theory has been top-notch. A little time out in the field and you should have the makings of a first-rate field biologist."

Cassie's palms were sweating. So far, Dr. Wells had sung the praises of every other person on the project. And he hadn't had to work very hard to do it. Yet she knew perfectly well she had nothing to contribute, that she was only along for the ride because her father had used his connections. She could feel her cheeks reddening as she braced herself for the uncomfortable silence she expected to follow, now that he'd rattled off everyone else's name.

"As for you, Cassie . . ."

She held her breath, meanwhile making a point of staring out the window of the van.

"I think you may be surprised this summer, not only by how much you learn, but also by how much you're able to add to the project."

She let out a sigh of relief.

"At any rate," said Dr. Wells, "I'd like to make this my official welcome. I promise that what's ahead will be one of the best educational experiences you've ever had—not to mention one of the most fun."

From where she sat—stuffed into a van with a single familiar face among a group of strangers, headed for one of the last uncivilized places on earth, one that happened to be five thousand miles from everything she'd ever known—Cassie had to admit she found Dr. Wells's promise hard to believe.

chapter
five

Pressing her face against the window of the plane, Laurel drew her breath in sharply. Nothing she had ever imagined, no daydream she'd ever constructed, had even begun to prepare her for her first glimpse of Alaska.

Slowly, the plane was descending over Turnagain Arm, the branch of Cook Inlet that ran south of Anchorage. It drifted down through the thick carpet of clouds that had been her only view since leaving Chicago seven hours earlier for the third and longest leg of their journey from Vermont. Suddenly a spectacular panorama stretched out before her.

The jagged coastline, a rich emerald green, formed sharp Vs that jutted out into muddy gray-blue water. Not far inland was a dense covering of trees that looked like velvet from the air. Everywhere tiny lakes dotted the landscape. Most dramatic, however, were the mountains. Huge dark gray masses of craggy rock cut through the ground, as forbidding as they were beautiful. Their tops were sprinkled with snow, such a pristine white that they shimmered in the pale sunlight.

"Look!" Laurel cried, her voice catching in her throat. "Isn't it the most . . . the most . . ."

"Amazing." Russ, sitting behind her, his face also pressed against the window, supplied the word for her.

"It's the only way to describe it. I've never seen any-thing so magnificent in my life."

"If you ask me," commented Mariah, "it looks like we're about to land on another planet."

"I don't remember anybody asking you," Trip said from across the aisle, "but you're right. It does look like we're hovering over Jupiter or Mars."

"That's Planet Earth, all right," said Dr. Wells. "Earth the way it looked before so-called civilization came along."

"I don't see any signs of life," said Cassie.

"There'd better be." Mariah, who'd been leaning over Russ to get a better view out the window, turned away and went back to her fashion magazine. "My hair dryer broke last night. If we don't find a drug store, I'm going to go around looking like the Bride of Franken-stein."

While Laurel had expected to be tired after the long trip, she was instead energized by finally having reached their destination. Even the ordeal of waiting for all their scientific gear and personal belongings at the baggage claim, renting a Jeep, and loading everything into it for the second time that day did little to dampen her spirits.

"We'll be driving directly to Wolf Lake, a few hours to the southwest," Dr. Wells informed them as they headed out of Anchorage Airport onto Seward High-way. "I'm anxious to get everyone settled as quickly as possible. I'd like to get started first thing tomorrow morning. We'll begin by laying fish traps, taking mea-surements of the lake, collecting plant specimens—"

"Tomorrow?" Mariah squawked.

"Don't tell me you've got something more important to do," Trip countered.

"I just figured we'd take a day or two to get settled. Unpack, go into town. . . ."

"Where we're going," said Dr. Wells, his voice reflecting his amusement, "there *is* no town. And getting unpacked should take you all of five minutes."

As they drove along the coast of the Kenai Peninsula, Laurel sat next to the window of the rented Jeep, her eyes wide as she eagerly took in her brand-new surroundings. She was awestruck by how wonderfully untouched Alaska was. The roads weren't lined with stores and houses, like they were back home. Instead, the two-lane highways cut through endless acres of fields and forests. In the distance was an incredibly beautiful and dramatic backdrop of craggy snow-covered mountains.

They drove past fields of colorful wildflowers, stretching on as far as the eye could see. They passed calm blue lakes that looked like pictures on a calendar. They rode by violent rivers in which the swirling water, tinged a deep shade of blue-green, was perfectly clear.

"Glacial melt," Dr. Wells explained as they gasped over the beauty of the Kenai River. "That's why the water's so pure—and such an unusual color."

At one point what little traffic there was slowed to a halt.

"What now?" Mariah demanded, craning her neck to see out the front of the car. "Gridlock?"

"Not quite." Dr. Wells was grinning. "Here in Alaska drivers brake for moose."

Sure enough, up ahead, a stately moose took her time strolling across the highway. She was easily one of the biggest animals Laurel had ever seen—certainly the largest she'd spotted in the wild. Even after the moose had made it to the other side of the road and stood munching on a low willow bush, the cars remained at a stop as onlookers took out their cameras.

It wasn't long before Laurel understood precisely

what Dr. Wells had meant about getting unpacked in five minutes. After a long drive along a winding dirt road that took them way off the main highway, the rented Jeep stopped with a lurch. A cloud of dust rose up all around. Fifty feet away was a crude log cabin, no more than twenty feet by twenty feet. It was compact and angular, with a slanted roof. Three steps led to a small front porch. On it were two propane tanks, a sign that a gas stove was inside. Pushed off to one side were large plastic jugs of water.

"Home, sweet home," said Dr. Wells. "Okay, everybody. Pile out."

Cassie swallowed so hard Laurel could hear her. Her panic only thinly masked, she cried, "You mean this is where we're supposed to *live* for the next six weeks?"

Mariah just stared. "You've got to be kidding. Somebody tell me this is nothing but a cruel joke."

"This is my fifth summer up here," said Dr. Wells. "I promise that after you make a few minor adjustments, you'll feel just as comfortable as you do in your own houses."

As Laurel climbed out of the Jeep and stood in front of the log cabin nestled in the woods that, as Dr. Wells said, was going to be her home for the rest of the summer, her reaction was quite different from that of the two girls standing on either side of her. To her, coming to a place like this meant having a lifelong fantasy finally come true.

It wasn't only the rustic structure that she would be living in that was responsible for the fluttering of her heart as she dragged her sleeping bag and her duffel bag up the rough wooden steps and onto the porch. Even more attractive was the idea of being completely surrounded by dense woods, a clear blue sky, and a hundred yards away, Wolf Lake. Civilization was far away.

Here, she was in the middle of the world the way it was meant to be.

Laurel pushed her way through the thick sheets of mosquito netting draped across the door. Once inside, it took her a few seconds to adjust to the dim light. The dark, wooden walls were dotted by small windows. The cabin was basically one good-sized room that had been divided up. In front was a common living space that included a sagging brown-plaid couch, a table and chairs, and a kitchen area with a sink and drain but no running water. Behind were two tiny back bedrooms, one on each side. Glancing up, she saw a loft that could be reached by a ladder. It was lighted by a single large window, its screen thick with rust.

Mariah came in and made a quick survey of her own. "I'm almost afraid to ask," she said in a strained voice, "but where's the bathroom?"

"The outhouse is off to the right, about a hundred feet into the woods," Dr. Wells replied matter-of-factly as he stepped inside. "Okay. Before everybody starts putting their stuff down, I'll give you your room assignments. Russ and Trip, you take the loft. I'll take the bedroom off to the left, the smaller of the two. Cassie, Laurel, and Mariah, you three'll be sharing the other back bedroom. In it are a set of bunk beds and a cot. You can battle out who gets which. But don't worry; with your sleeping bags spread out on them, you should all be pretty comfortable."

"Three to a room?" Mariah protested.

"Hey," said Trip, brightening, "if any of you ladies feels too crowded, you're welcome to—"

"Spare us," Laurel broke in. "I'm sure we'll manage just fine."

She glanced over at Cassie, wanting to give her an encouraging smile. But the woeful look on her best

friend's face told her it would take a lot more than that
to cheer her up.

Dr. Wells had been correct in his assessment of how
long it would take everyone to unpack. Spreading out
her sleeping bag on the top bunk and hanging some of
her clothes up on the hooks on the wall took Laurel less
than five minutes. Leaving Cassie to wrestle with her
sleeping bag on the bottom bunk and Mariah to agonize
over how little storage space there was for all the
clothes she'd brought, she went into the kitchen area to
find something to drink.

Dr. Wells had beat her there. "I've mixed up a pitcher
of iced tea," he informed her cheerfully. "We even have
ice. That refrigerator might be small, but thanks to the
magic of propane it works as well as any other."

Laurel accepted the cold drink he offered. Perching on
the edge of the couch, she was about to ask him about the
first steps the team would be taking the following morning when a stranger's voice called, "Knock, knock!"

Standing in the doorway, holding back the mosquito
netting, was a tall, gaunt man with a ragged beard and
bright blue eyes. At his side was a small boy, probably
no older than eight or nine. Like his father, his dark
blond hair looked as if it could use a trim. His blue eyes
were also exact copies of the older man's. One thing
that was noticeably different, however, was the scattering of freckles across his nose and cheeks.

"I'm John Torvold, the station manager of the Wolf
Lake Preserve. And this is Danny. Is Dr. Wells here?"

"I'm right here, John." He emerged from the kitchen
area, his own glass of iced tea in hand.

"Ethan! Great to see you!" The two men exchanged
a hearty handshake.

"Same here." Dr. Wells tousled Danny's hair. "Hey, Danny. How's that insect collection going?"

The little boy looked surprised. "You remembered!"

"Of course I remembered," said Dr. Wells. "You've got one of the most impressive collections I've ever seen."

Danny was beaming. "I've got more than a hundred species!" he reported proudly.

The sound of footsteps out on the front porch caused them all to look out. A woman in jeans and a T-shirt was hovering behind them, smiling shyly.

"Come on in, Lucy," said John. "Dr. Wells is back— and he's brought a whole new group of students."

The sound of unrecognizable voices brought the others out of the sleeping areas and into the front room.

"Let me introduce all of you," Dr. Wells said, suddenly sounding strangely formal. "Lucy and John Torvold, meet Laurel Adams, Cassie Davis, Trip Raynor, Mariah Burke, and Russ Corcoran. John and Lucy take care of things here on the preserve. Their son, Danny, knows more about this place than anybody in the world."

"I learned a whole bunch of new stuff, too!" the boy asserted, wearing a wide grin.

"There's somebody else living on the preserve," said John. "Jim Whitehorse helps me with some of the heavy work around here. He's kind of a loner, living off in the woods in his own cabin. In fact, you probably won't be seeing very much of him."

Danny's eyes had grown wide. "He's a big, scary-looking guy. Every time I see him, I *run*!"

His father chuckled, meanwhile placing a comforting hand on the boy's shoulder. "There's no reason to be afraid of Whitehorse," he insisted. "He's just the kind of person who likes to keep to himself, that's all."

"Anything else we need to know?" asked Dr. Wells.

John and Lucy exchanged nervous glances. Laurel found herself growing uncomfortable.

"There is one thing we'd better warn you about," John Torvold said slowly.

"You mean the bears, Dad?" said Danny.

Cassie gasped. "Bears!"

"You're joking, right?" Mariah said at the same time.

As for Trip, his face had lit up. "Cool!" he breathed.

"We've seen signs of the bears coming closer to the cabins than ever before," Danny informed them excitedly. "We actually saw paw prints in the dirt." Proudly he added, "I'm the one who found them."

Cassie's blue eyes were wide. "I thought I'd heard they don't bother humans if the humans don't bother them."

"They usually don't," said John. "Most of the time, when they pick up the scent of a human—and they have an excellent sense of smell—they take off in the opposite direction. And if you ever come across one while you're out in the woods, he'll probably just sniff you and then leave you alone."

" 'Most of the time'? 'Probably'?" Cassie swallowed hard. "If this is supposed to make me feel better, it's not working."

"The truth of the matter," Lucy Torvold interjected, "is that Cassie's right to be cautious. See that wall over there?"

The group looked over in the direction she'd indicated. Laurel noticed that the wood along one section did look newer than the rest.

"A few years back, a bear chewed a hole through that wall and came right in. He didn't even bother with the door."

"He must have been looking for food," said Laurel.

"Not necessarily," said John. "Sure, people tend to say that. But I've seen bears come into a cabin even when there was no food."

"I'm sure this won't come up," Russ said evenly, choosing his words carefully, "but what do you recommend we do if a bear ever does come into the cabin?"

"Make as much noise as you can," said Lucy. "Yell, wave your arms, rattle pots and pans. . . . Chances are, that'll scare him off."

"H-how big do these bears get?" asked Cassie

"The Alaskan brown bear—the grizzly—is the largest meat-eating animal living on land," Trip volunteered.

"They get to be eight or nine feet long," Russ added. "And they can weigh more than fifteen hundred pounds."

"Fifteen *hundred*?" Cassie gulped. "They're as big as cars!"

"Fortunately, they're not quite as fast," said Trip. "Although twenty or twenty-five miles per hour isn't bad."

"I don't want to have any run-ins with bears any more than the rest of you," said Laurel, "but I certainly wouldn't mind seeing one."

"They're beautiful animals," Trip agreed.

"Maybe too beautiful for their own good," John Torvold muttered, more to himself than to the others.

"What do you mean?" asked Mariah.

He paused a moment, as if wondering whether or not to go ahead and say what he was thinking. "We've been having problems with poachers. People coming around and killing bears illegally."

"What for?" Cassie asked.

"Probably for nothing more than the sheer joy of killing," Mariah replied dryly.

"It's true that some of them are hunters," John explained. "Actually, it's perfectly legal to kill during the season. The Department of Fish and Game sets aside a month in the spring and a month in the fall when bear hides are at their peak. In the summer, the hides aren't much good. The bears are shedding, so their fur's not full.

"It's only during the legal hunting season that hunters can get themselves what we call 'a good prime bear.' Fish and Game has no problem with that, as long as the hunter applies for a license first and then abides by all the laws."

"What are those?" asked Trip.

"First of all, it's against the law to kill a cub or a sow with cubs. Second, when a hunter does kill a bear, he has to bring in the skull and the hide. The biologists check it out—the size, the condition of the fur, the time of the year it's been killed. All that's to help us regulate the season.

"Aside from the time of the year and the kind of bear a hunter's allowed to kill, we also regulate how it's done."

Mariah shrugged. "Don't the hunters just go out and shoot with rifles?"

"Basically. That's your average hunter, anyway. But some people want to turn what's meant to be a sport into a business. The main regulation is against using aircraft to get bears. There are professional guides, people who know their way around up here. They're licensed pilots who own their own supercubs, little PA-18s that can land on mountaintops or clearings. These planes have big wheels—tundra wheels—or else skis for landing on snow in the spring. They take people up into the mountains and drop them off.

"All that's fine. It's when they use two planes that they're breaking the law. The way it works is, they track a bear from the air, looking for prints on the trail or in the snow. Once they locate him, one drives him toward the other plane, where he gets shot. The bottom line is that it's illegal to 'chase and herd.' "

"Then, of course," Lucy Torvold interjected, "there are people who kill a bear to get its claws and its gallbladder."

"That's ridiculous," Cassie cried. "Killing a huge animal for two small parts—"

"Sure it's ridiculous—to you and me." John frowned. "But some people'd do anything to make a buck. You see, they can sell a bear gallbladder. In certain Asian cultures, it's believed to be an aphrodisiac—something that makes people feel romantic. As for the claws, they're sold to people who wear them around their neck or keep them on their desk, just for show."

Laurel gasped. "Unbelievable!"

"It's even more unbelievable since a bear gallbladder's worth less than a hundred dollars. Still, it happens more often than you'd think. And, as I said, lately it's been happening around Wolf Lake. In the past few weeks, I came across three illegal kills."

"Are you sure?" asked Laurel.

"Aside from the time of year, you can usually tell when somebody's killed a bear illegally because he'll cover up the remains with willow branches and leave it to rot. See, a stripped carcass is white, and it's easy for a plane to spot. If you're somebody who wants to keep your little secret safe, you've got to hide it."

"Just as long as all this is going on in the woods—and not around here," Mariah commented with a shudder. "As far as I'm concerned, the less I see or even hear about bears, the better."

"I suppose we're well stocked with pepper spray, just in case," Russ said matter-of-factly.

"Oh, yes," said Lucy. "There are a few cans on that shelf. Help yourselves."

"Pepper spray?" Cassie repeated, puzzled. "What's that?"

"A spray can filled with hot pepper," Trip explained, his attitude as casual as Russ's. "Whenever you go out into the woods, make sure you bring it. If a bear comes close, spray it into his eyes."

Mariah stared at him, her hands on her hips. "You're joking, right? I mean, you're not really advising us to resort to hand-to-hand combat with a monster the size of Godzilla, are you?"

Trip shrugged. "You can always run. Of course, any grizzly worth his salt can outrun you. Not to mention the fact that as soon as he sees you take off, he'll assume you're a tasty morsel that'll make the perfect lunch."

"Great," Mariah muttered. She flopped down on the couch, letting out a loud sigh. "Welcome to Alaska."

"What a nightmare!" Cassie sobbed. She threw her gear onto the lumpy bed, then sank onto its edge with her head in her hands. "Oh, Laurel! How am I ever going to get through the next six weeks?"

"It's not so bad," Laurel insisted. She sat down next to her, patting her comfortingly on the shoulder.

"*Bad!* I don't know which part is the *worst*! First of all, just look at this place!" Cassie cried. "It looks like . . . it looks like something a kid built out of Lincoln Logs!"

Laurel couldn't help smiling. "It's a lot more substantial than that. Besides, toys don't come equipped with propane stoves and hurricane lamps and fully-functioning refrigerators."

"Did you see what we're supposed to use for a bathroom?"

"Outhouses don't exactly have the reputation of being luxurious."

"But it *smells*! And there are so many mosquitoes I could hardly see." Cassie shuddered. "I couldn't even close the door. I tried, but it was dark. There's no electricity in there!"

"Still, you've got to admit it offers a terrific view of the lake," Laurel joked.

Cassie was anything but amused. "Oh, Laurel, how am I ever going to stand it?" she wailed. "You know as well as I do that coming here wasn't my idea. I was all set for a relaxing summer, working the cash register in some air-conditioned store, spending every spare moment I could find drawing and painting." She took a deep breath, hoping her voice would stop wavering. "D-do you think if I told my parents what it's really like here, they'd let me go home?"

Laurel slung a sisterly arm around her friend. "Come on, Cassie. It won't be so bad. Before you know it, this place'll seem like home. It'll be fun. Sleeping in a log cabin, living on a lake . . . doesn't the idea of a real-life adventure appeal to you at all?"

Cassie's only response was a grimace.

"Okay. Then at least try to make the best of it. Sure, living in the woods like this will be more of a challenge than spending the summer standing behind the counter in a store. But at least we have each other."

Cassie tried to smile, without much success. "Maybe if it were just you and me, it wouldn't be so bad. But I don't know how I'm ever going to spend an entire summer with Mariah."

"Oh, after a few days, the three of us will probably be the best of friends." Laurel waved her hand in the air. "You'd be surprised how common experience brings people together. Besides, Russ seems kind of nice, don't you think?"

Cassie gave a halfhearted shrug. "He's all right, I guess."

"And Trip ... well, as I said, people change once they get to know each other. Besides, I think Dr. Wells is great, don't you?"

"Yeah, he seems pretty cool." Cassie took a deep breath. "But what about that weird guy John told us about? I'm not exactly crazy about the idea of him wandering around in the woods out there." She picked at imaginary pieces of lint on the right knee of her jeans. "He reminds me of Big Foot."

Laurel laughed. "Maybe he is. That would certainly explain *that* legend. But seriously, Cassie, I'm sure he's not going to bother us. The way John described him, he didn't exactly impress me as somebody who's going to be coming around here day and night, asking to borrow a cup of sugar."

"What about the bears?" Cassie grumbled. "I bet you can't say the same for them."

Laurel hesitated, biting her lip pensively as she stared at the floor. "Well, the bears are a real danger. I can't deny that. We just have to be careful and take all the precautions the Torvolds told us about.

"I know all this is a bit of a shock for you, Cassie. I agree with you that Alaska isn't like anyplace else I've ever seen. But I'd bet anything that in a couple of days, this place will feel like home, just like Dr. Wells promised. Without cable TV, of course."

Cassie could feel some of her fears melting away. Laurel sounded so certain that things weren't that bad. She actually seemed to *like* it here.

Of course, Laurel is Laurel, Cassie reminded herself.

She is my best friend, but her idea of a good time has always seemed kind of strange to me. I mean, traipsing through the woods, risking bug bites and poison ivy and who even knows what else? Holing up in a lab for hours on end glued to a microscope? Memorizing the names of parts of plants and animals as if they really mattered?

Even so, Cassie was willing to give Laurel the benefit of the doubt, to buy in to her claim that somehow, through some power she couldn't quite comprehend, she was actually going to get through this summer.

After all, she had very little choice.

chapter
six

Laurel stepped out of the dimly-lit cabin and was greeted by the early morning sun, already high in the pale Alaskan sky. She pushed up the sleeves of the long-sleeved T-shirt she wore with a pair of jeans, raising her face toward the sun's welcoming rays.

Even though she was alone, she smiled. All around her, the world was coming alive with the new day. The forest was rich with color, a breathtaking mosaic of greens and browns. Hidden in the dense leaves of the trees were birds, fluttering through the branches, calling to each other with sweet chirping sounds. Even the buzzing mosquitoes seemed especially alert on this fine June morning.

As she stood outside the cabin, what struck her even more than the sights and sounds was the fragrance. The thick growth of leaves, still moist with dew; the damp soil beneath her feet; the fresh, clear air. . . . Laurel took a deep breath, eagerly drawing it all in. She was experiencing a sense of contentment she couldn't remember having felt in a very long time.

She was startled by the unexpected sound of Dr. Wells's voice. "It's beautiful out here, isn't it?"

Her self-consciousness over having been caught off guard only lasted a moment. "It's pretty incredible," she agreed. "In a way being here is like taking a trip back in time, seeing the world the way it must have looked millions of years ago. No roads, no shopping centers . . . not a single candy wrapper or cigarette butt lying on the ground."

"You can experience complete peace up here," said Dr. Wells. "Kind of makes you wish you'd never have to return to civilization again, doesn't it?"

Before she had a chance to respond, the stillness around them was interrupted by a loud thumping. Laurel turned and saw Mariah and Trip coming out of the cabin, dragging fish traps, a giant cooler, and a few other assorted items onto the porch.

"Why do we have to be the packhorses?" Mariah grumbled. "This is the 1990s. Why can't we take advantage of the invention of the wheel? Right now I'd kill for a wagon or a . . . a wheelbarrow or—"

"It's only a couple of hundred feet from here to the lake," Trip returned. "Besides, the path's too narrow and bumpy for a wheelbarrow. Too bad your chauffeur's not here."

"So much for complete peace," Laurel commented to Dr. Wells, smiling wryly. She turned toward Trip and Mariah. "Let me help you get that stuff down to the canoes."

Picking up as much as she could of the equipment the others had hauled out of the cabin, Laurel headed down the path. She was looking forward eagerly to her first day out on the lake and getting started on the research that had brought them all up here in the first place. She'd only gone a few paces when she felt someone's hand on her shoulder.

"Hello, Trip," she said, shrugging away from him. "All set for today? I have a feeling we've got a lot of hard work ahead of us."

"Great. Being out on the lake together will give you and me a chance to get to know each other better."

Laurel cast him a wary look, peering over the awkward metal fish traps she was carrying. "Look, Trip. There's one thing you and I had better get straight from the very beginning. I'm here to learn—and nothing more."

"Hey, you know what they say—'All work and no play ...'"

"Read my lips. I came to Alaska to work, not to socialize."

"You know, Laurel, there's something I can't quite figure out." Trip took a step backward, his blue eyes narrowing as he looked her up and down.

"What's that?"

"Any girl as pretty as you is bound to have a boyfriend. And why this boyfriend of yours would ever agree to let you go away for practically the whole summer is beyond me."

Laurel could feel her blood starting to boil. "In the first place," she said as evenly as she could, "my personal life is none of your business. In the second place, I would never let a boyfriend—or anybody else, for that matter—stand in the way of something that really mattered to me, something like this trip. In the third place, the idea of a boyfriend 'letting' me do anything is so—so *primitive* that I can hardly believe you actually had the nerve to bring it up. In the fourth place—"

Trip chuckled. "I get your point."

"I'm not sure about that."

"Sure I do. You're one of those girls who likes to play hard to get." Trip threw back his head, his hollow laugh echoing through the woods.

Laurel opened her mouth to reply, then quickly snapped it shut. What was the point? Arguing with Trip would accomplish nothing besides convincing him that he was right in believing she was simply "playing hard to get." The best thing to do, she decided, was simply to ignore him.

"Okay, everybody," Dr. Wells announced once the group had reached the shore. By that point, Russ had joined them, with Cassie straggling a few paces behind. "We're going out in three canoes today. That means two people per canoe."

"Oh, goody," muttered Mariah. She smoothed the stylishly baggy white jeans she was wearing with a Hawaiian print blouse and large enameled earrings shaped like lush tropical flowers. "The buddy system."

"There are a few things I want to mention," Dr. Wells continued. "Since this is our first day out, I'll be coming along with you to make sure there are no complications. After I'm confident you can manage on your own, I'll often stay behind and process the collections, analyze data, or just plan our work.

"Before we start, I want to make sure everyone's clear about what it is we hope to accomplish. Over the next few weeks, we'll be taking an inventory of the plants and the animals in and around Wolf Lake. Even though our main goal for today is to get fish traps in the water in all the different sections of the lake, it wouldn't be a bad idea to start collecting a few water samples. Russ has a lot of experience in that area. He and I will show you how to use the Van Doren sampler.

"Aside from setting fish traps and collecting water samples, begin looking out for different varieties of birds and insects. The same goes for herbarium specimens."

"He means plants," Trip interjected.

Mariah rolled her eyes.

Dr. Wells ignored them both. "We'll make a full-scale effort to take cuttings and get them in plant presses later on. For now, you can start collecting specimens as you come across them. That way, you'll already have a head start when we start our routine surveys—what we call transects."

Dr. Wells looked around at his research team, standing around him in a loose circle. "Okay. If there aren't any questions, let's get started."

He'd barely gotten the words out when Cassie rushed over to Laurel. "You'll share a canoe with me, won't you?" she asked anxiously.

Looking at the outfit she'd chosen to wear that day, it was all Laurel could do to keep from bursting out laughing. Cassie was covered from head to foot. With her jeans she had on a long-sleeved shirt, the cuffs tightly fastened, the buttons done up all the way. Her feet were covered with rubber shoes that laced up her ankles. She wore a pair of cotton gardening gloves on her hands and a floppy canvas fisherman's hat on her head. Around her neck was a bright red bandanna. As if all that weren't enough, her nose and cheeks were white, smeared with a thick coating of zinc oxide.

"Exactly what are you anticipating out there today, Cassie?" Laurel asked as gently as she could.

"Everything! Mosquitoes, sunburn—"

"Cassie's right to be cautious," Dr. Wells interrupted. "Sunburn can be a real problem—especially on the water, where the sun's rays are reflected off the surface of the lake." From his knapsack he pulled out two bottles. The first was a large plastic bottle of sunblock, the second Cutter's mosquito repellent. "The mosquitoes are no fun, either. Pass both of these around—and be generous. The first day out is always the worst."

"I'll pass, thanks," Trip called over his shoulder. He was bent over one of the canoes, loading equipment.

"I highly recommend a good dose of each," said Dr. Wells. "That includes you, Trip. Your coloring is pretty fair. I know people don't generally think of Alaska as the sunburn capital of the world, but—"

"If you don't mind, I'll take my chances."

Dr. Wells hesitated a moment, then shrugged. "I guess some lessons simply have to be learned the hard way." He handed both bottles to Mariah. "Okay, let's pair off, two per canoe."

"Laurel and I are going together," Cassie piped up.

"You do know your way around a canoe, don't you?" Dr. Wells asked Laurel.

When she nodded, he turned his attention to the others. "It makes sense to have at least one person in each boat who knows what he or she is doing. Mariah, do you have any experience with canoes?"

"Yeah, right," Trip said under his breath. "Riding the rapids is the second most popular pastime in Beverly Hills—after shopping for designer toothbrushes on Rodeo Drive, that is."

"That's enough, Trip," Dr. Wells said sternly. "Mariah, you pair up with Russ. That'll put Trip and me in the last canoe."

As Laurel pulled on her orange flotation jacket, standing next to the boat that had been designated as the one she and Cassie were to share, she said, "I'll take the front. That'll make it easier to steer. Besides, it'll help you learn—Cassie, what *is* all that?"

She watched in amazement as Cassie hauled a huge plastic shopping bag into the canoe, doing her best to tuck it between her feet.

Cassie froze. "Nothing, really. Just some stuff I thought I might need."

"What kind of stuff? Dr. Wells brought along enough supplies and equipment for the entire day."

"Just some . . . extra provisions."

"You mean food?"

In response to her nod, Laurel said, "But Cassie, we're already dragging along enough food for a small army."

Cassie pushed her bag back further, meanwhile keeping her eyes down. "I'm afraid I might get hungry. These are just some cookies and things I brought from home."

Laurel resisted the temptation to engage in an argument she suspected she could never win. Instead, she turned her attention to the lake that stretched ahead, waiting to be explored.

The day couldn't have been more delightful nor the mood more upbeat as the group set out in the three canoes. The six paddles sent out waves of ripples, intermingling in kaleidoscopic patterns on the glassy surface of the lake as the canoes skimmed smoothly across the water. To her left, Laurel could see Dr. Wells and Trip, their boat already far ahead. Off to the right, Russ was paddling with ease, his canoe close to hers. Mariah, sitting behind him, struggled with her paddle, her face twisted into a grimace as she wrestled with the water.

Laurel slowed down so that she and Cassie were bringing up the rear. She wanted a chance to enjoy her surroundings—even though she suspected her copilot, panting behind her, was working much too hard to be having any fun.

"How're you doing back there?" she called over her shoulder.

"Fine," Cassie puffed. "This is a lot more work than I thought. In the movies, it always looks so easy."

"Make sure your paddle is straight up and down as you dip it into the water—like this."

"It's no use," Cassie insisted. "I'll never get the hang of this. It's too hard."

Once again Laurel decided not to argue. In the long silence that followed, she contentedly drifted back into her reverie, shutting out all thoughts except for her appreciation of the moment. She luxuriated in the feeling of the warm sun on the back of her neck, the cool breeze rising up off the lake as their canoe veered off to the left, following Dr. Wells's lead. . . .

"Laurel?"

"Yes, Cassie?"

"I've been meaning to ask you something kind of . . . personal."

The strain in Cassie's voice immediately put Laurel on guard. "Shoot."

A few more seconds passed before Cassie asked, "Are you interested in Trip?"

Laurel was so shocked by her question that she nearly dropped her paddle into the lake. "What on earth are you talking about? Me . . . interested in that jerk? You've got to be kidding! I don't think I've ever met someone with a male ego that big. In fact, it's all I can do to keep from giving him a piece of my mind. But since we all have to work together, I figure that wouldn't do anybody any good." Peeking at Cassie over her shoulder, she added, "Why do you ask?"

"Oh, I don't know," Cassie said. "I guess I just noticed the two of you hanging out together a lot."

Suddenly another thought occurred to Laurel. "Don't tell me you. . . ." In a gentler voice, she asked, "How about you? What do you think of Trip?"

"Oh, he's okay, I guess," Cassie replied, her tone just a bit too casual.

Laurel was tempted to ask more questions—a lot more questions. While she was debating whether or not that was wise, a shriek suddenly cut through the tranquil silence of the lake.

She turned and saw a look of horror on Mariah's face.

"A bear!" she screeched. "I just saw a bear!"

chapter
seven

While Laurel told herself over and over again that there was probably nothing to be afraid of, she was gripped by a fear unlike any she'd ever known before. She sat frozen in her canoe, her heart pounding, her mouth dry, her stomach in a tight knot. Glancing down, she saw that she was holding her wooden paddle so tightly that her knuckles had turned white.

"Calm down," Dr. Wells instructed the group, his voice surprisingly calm. "You heard what John Torvold said. If there really is a bear on shore, he's probably more frightened of us than we are of him."

"I knew coming on this stupid trip was a mistake!" Mariah cried. "We've got to get out of here—fast!"

Cassie's voice was reduced to a whimper as she cried, "He won't come into the water after us ... will he?"

Before anyone had a chance to answer, Russ cried, "That's no bear! It's a man!"

Sure enough, a long figure had suddenly emerged from the woods and into the dense growth of long reedy grass edging that portion of the lake. Laurel let out a deep sigh of relief.

While she could see how someone with an overly active imagination could have been confused about the identity of the large, hulking mass moving through the shadows, in full view it was clear that it was, indeed, a man. He was tall and broad shouldered, with jet black hair, dark leathery skin, and piercing eyes that burned like two pieces of coal. He was dressed in ill-fitting jeans and an oversize jacket made of coarse red-plaid wool. Slung over his shoulder was a rifle, and a long knife in a sheath hung down from his belt.

The man stood near the shore, gazing out in their direction. But Laurel grew uncomfortable as she realized he wasn't looking at them, but rather past them, off into the distance. It was as if as far as he was concerned, they didn't even exist.

"That must be Jim Whitehorse," said Russ, shielding his eyes with his hand. "The man John Torvold told us about."

"For heaven's sake, Mariah," Trip said coldly. "He's wearing a red-plaid jacket. How could you ever have mistaken him for a bear?"

"I can't help it if I thought he was an animal!" Mariah insisted. "The way he suddenly came rushing toward us—"

"That man doesn't look as if he's rushed toward anything in a couple of decades," Russ grumbled.

"Well, it was a mistake anybody could have made." Mariah was now pouting. "Besides, if it really had turned out to be a bear, you'd all be glad I'd been such a good scout."

"If it really was a bear," Trip muttered, "we'd all be lunch meat."

Dr. Wells said nothing. Instead, he concentrated on paddling the canoe he and Trip shared in Jim Whitehorse's direction.

"Hello!" he called.

The expression on the man's face didn't change. Instead, he continued staring out across the lake.

"I'm Ethan Wells. This is my field crew. We're up here from Vermont for the summer, studying the natural history of the area." When he still got no response, Dr. Wells added, "You must be Jim Whitehorse."

Slowly the man's eyes moved in their direction. "I'm Whitehorse," the man replied.

"John Torvold told us we might be running into you. We'll pretty much be keeping to ourselves, but if you find that we're getting in your way, please feel free—"

He never did finish his sentence. Whitehorse had already turned and headed back toward the woods.

"He's friendly," Mariah muttered.

"As far as I'm concerned," Cassie retorted, "the further away he stays from me, the better. That guy gives me the creeps!"

Laurel just stared. She couldn't help wondering about him. What kind of man chose to live by himself, having so little contact with the rest of the human race? How had he come to live here on the edge of Wolf Lake? Was he ever lonely, or was it possible for someone to live in nearly complete isolation?

Despite her curiosity, she had a feeling she'd never find out the answers to any of her questions. Jim Whitehorse was forgotten as she turned her attention to the task at hand: maneuvering her canoe through the tall grass, into a tiny inlet that Dr. Wells had just identified as the ideal place to start setting fish traps.

For the rest of the day, she and the others worked steadily. They dropped metal minnow traps to the bottom of the lake, then fastened their long strings to the shore by tying them to the branches of sturdy bushes or thick clumps of grass with fluorescent tape. Their cone-shaped interiors made it easy for fish to swim in, but virtually impossible for them to find their way out. In twenty-four hours, Dr. Wells informed them, the group would come back and check the traps to see what kind of fish were living in the different sections of the lake.

Collecting water samples was a little more complicated. Still, it wasn't long before Laurel and the others had mastered the technique. First they estimated the depth of the lake at various spots, using a rope that was marked at one-meter intervals and had a rock attached to the end. Then they used a mechanism called a Van Doren sampler to collect water at different depths.

The hours flew by. Laurel was astonished when Dr. Wells suddenly announced, "It's almost nine. We'd better head back and start thinking about dinner."

"Nine?" Laurel gasped. "Nine o'clock?"

Cassie cast her an odd look. "For goodness' sake, Laurel. I've been watching the clock for hours. I thought we'd never get around to eating."

Laurel wasn't about to comment on the four candy bars she'd watched her put away over the course of the afternoon—or the handful of cookies Cassie had helped herself to around six.

It wasn't until the caravan of canoes was nearing the edge of the lakeshore and the roof of the log cabin came into sight that Laurel realized how tired she was. She and the others had put in more than fourteen hours on the lake. Everyone was tired; she could tell from the silence that hung heavily over the group. The only sound, aside from the call of distant birds, the buzz of insects, and occasionally, the lonely cry of a loon, was that made by the paddles as they cut through the surface of the water.

Yet as the six of them hauled the canoes on shore and began unloading them, Laurel was struck by the fact that Trip was moving particularly slowly. Glancing over at him, she saw that it was more than fatigue that made him so quiet.

His face, neck, and arms were beet red.

"Trip!" she exclaimed. "You're burned!"

"Oh, it's nothing," he mumbled. "I just got a little too much sun, that's all."

But Dr. Wells wasn't quite as casual. Peering at Trip, he said, "Whoa. You've got a bad sunburn, pal. Better plan on spending tomorrow indoors."

"No way!" he protested.

"I'm in charge here," Dr. Wells said, his tone unusually sharp. "The last thing I need up here is a bad case of sun poisoning simply because you weren't willing to follow a couple of simple rules. I've got something you can put on that back at the cabin."

"I don't need to—okay, fine."

Trip gritted his teeth as he applied the thick white cream Dr. Wells insisted he use. He seemed considerably more relaxed once the ointment covered his burned skin.

"We'll let you off the hook—this time," Mariah informed him as she set the table. "Tonight, you're off dinner duty. But as soon as you fade from fire-engine red to tomato red—"

"You're too kind," Trip shot back from the couch, where he was sprawled out. "Heart of gold."

It wasn't until dinner was on the table that Laurel realized how famished she was. She ate her fill of food that tasted better than any she'd ever had before. Afterward, she was still tired. Yet while her muscles were sore, knowing that she'd put in a full day of hard work gave her a feeling of great satisfaction. If her first day was any indication of what lay ahead, her stay in Alaska was going to be all that she'd ever hoped for.

Dr. Wells had been correct in his assertion that it would take at least a full day for Trip's sunburn to heal enough for him to go outside. The next morning, his skin was still dangerously red.

"If I wear a long-sleeved shirt, I'll be fine," he insisted over breakfast.

"Sorry, Trip." Dr. Wells's tone was firm. "I'm responsible for you while you're up here. You're staying indoors today, and that's final."

"Don't worry about being lonely," Mariah said sweetly. "Russ and I are taking the sweep nets out into the woods to collect insects. I promise we'll stop in every couple of hours so our specimens can visit."

"Trip won't have to stay here by himself," said Dr. Wells. "Laurel, I'd like you to stay in the cabin with him this morning—at least for a few hours. That burn is severe, and I don't want him left alone. Besides, I want you to start keying out the plant specimens we collected yesterday."

"What does that mean?" asked Cassie, glancing up from her plate, piled high with eggs and toast.

"It's a system for identifying unknown aquatic species," Russ explained patiently. "First you get hold of Hulten's *Flora of Alaska and Neighboring Territories*. It's kind of like a puzzle. The guide gives questions like, 'Are the petals joined . . . or not joined? If they are, go to A. If they're not, go to B.' Eventually, you decide what you think you've got and you compare it to the description for that species."

"Trip," said Dr. Wells, "you can make yourself useful by reading the key aloud while Laurel checks the specimens. The microscope's in my room. You'll need it to examine the tiny flowers of some of the plants."

"Sounds like fun," Cassie observed.

It would be fun. Even so, Laurel would have much preferred going out into the woods with the others. Still, identifying the species of plants they'd collected so far was necessary work, an important element of the research they'd come up here to do. If Trip needed a baby-sitter, it made sense for both jobs to get done at the same time.

After cleanup, the others took off, Mariah once again dressed like a model, Cassie dressed in her combat outfit. When they were gone, Laurel sat down at the table, ready to throw herself into the morning's project.

Behind her, lying sprawled across the couch with his arms folded underneath his head, Trip cleared his throat loudly.

"I sure feel stupid, getting burned like this," he said.

She resisted the temptation to agree. Instead, in as soothing a voice as she could manage, Laurel said, "If there's anything I can do to help—"

"As a matter of fact, there is. I feel so parched. I'd really appreciate a glass of water."

"No problem." Laurel got up from the table and poured a glassful of the bottled water on the counter. "Here you go. If there's anything else—"

"Since you offered, another pillow wouldn't hurt."

"Another pillow? Sure." Laurel climbed up the ladder, retrieved a pillow from the loft, and handed it to Trip.

"Maybe you could tuck it under my head?"

Laurel hesitated.

"Gosh, my face feels like it's on fire," Trip suddenly said, closing his eyes. "I don't think I've ever felt this terrible in my life."

"Here, maybe having your head higher will help." Gently Laurel lifted his head, cradling it in one arm as she tucked the second pillow underneath.

"You know what else would help," he said, his eyes snapping open. "Another coat of that lotion."

"It already seems pretty thick—"

"This sunburn is so painful, Laurel. I hope you never have to go through anything like this."

Dutifully Laurel took the bottle of lotion off the table, poured a dollop into the palm of her hand, and began smearing it lightly over Trip's face. "Does that hurt?" she asked nervously. "I wouldn't want to rub too hard. . . ."

"You're doing fine. Just fine." Trip closed his eyes once again. But this time, the look on his face was one of absolute contentment. "Now my neck . . ."

After pouring more lotion into her hand, Laurel continued her gentle massaging of Trip's reddened skin. "Ah, that feels so good," he said with a sigh. "You know, Laurel, it was worth getting the worst sunburn of my life, just to have you touch me like that—"

Laurel froze. "You creep! This isn't designed to help your sunburn at all, is it? You're just taking advantage of this situation to—"

"Oh, come on, Laurel. You played into it without a protest. I know you're attracted to me. Maybe you're not ready to admit it yet, but—" He reached for her hand, clasping it in his. "I think you and I would be really good together. If only you'd quit this little game of yours—"

"Let me go, Trip. Stop!"

"You're such a tease, Laurel. Pretty girls like you are always—"

"Cut it out!"

"Everything okay in here?"

The unexpected sound of a voice caused them both to turn. Glancing up, they saw a stranger standing in the doorway of the cabin. Trip immediately dropped Laurel's hand.

"I couldn't tell if you two were playing around or—or something else."

"Your timing's perfect," Laurel assured the man, standing up and smoothing her clothes. Turning back to Trip, she hissed, "If you ever try anything like that again, I'll do everything I possibly can to get you thrown off this project. You'll be shipped home so fast you won't have a chance to pack."

"Yeah, right," Trip returned. "As if Dr. Wells could manage without me."

"I'm sure he'd find a way."

Trip just laughed. "I'm going out," he called over his shoulder as he jumped off the couch and headed for the door. "Don't worry; I'll stay in the shade." He strode out of the cabin, vanishing behind the thick layer of mosquito netting. For the second time that day, she let out a deep sigh of relief.

"Are you all right?" The man's face was tense with concern.

"I'm fine," Laurel assured him. "But thanks for coming in. Fighting off Casanova was starting to get a little tricky."

"I'm Ben Seeger." Wearing a friendly smile, the man held out his hand. "I work for Fish and Game in Anchorage."

"I'm Laurel Adams." She shook his hand, meanwhile studying him. He was probably in his late thirties, she guessed, with hazel eyes and dark brown hair that was just beginning to gray at the temples. "I guess I owe you a big fat thank you."

"Glad I could be of service. Especially where an idiot like that is concerned."

Laurel shook her head. "The really sad part is that Trip is an excellent scientist. He knows so much. It's just that his ego is as big as . . . as big as the entire state of Alaska."

The man smiled. "If he's really serious about science, that kind of attitude is going to get in his way."

The mosquito netting was swept aside abruptly as Dr. Wells stormed into the cabin. "Where does Trip think he's going?" He stopped when he caught sight of Ben Seeger. "Ben! What a nice surprise!"

As the two men shook hands, Dr. Wells asked Laurel, "Have you two met? Ben is with the Alaska Department of Fish and Game. He used to be the game warden in these parts, but since he's been promoted he spends more time sitting behind a desk pushing papers than tromping around in the wilds."

Ben laughed. "That's what happens when you're given an official-sounding title like Enforcement Coordinator."

"Ben's been a great help to me during the years I've been coming up to do research," Dr. Wells explained.

"I heard you'd come up again, Ethan, this time with a field crew."

"We got in a couple of days ago. I appreciate your stopping in to say hello."

"Actually," said Ben, "I'm here on official business." In response to Dr. Wells's look of confusion, he went on, "The Torvolds have reported a couple of bear poachings. I'm here to check them out."

"Any clues as to who's behind them?"

Ben shook his head. "I'm not particularly optimistic, either. The guys who engage in this kind of thing are experts—and, frankly, our resources are too limited to give such incidents the full-scale investigation they deserve. I hate to say it, but chances are we'll never find out who the poachers are."

"That means you won't be able to put a stop to it, either," Laurel commented.

"I'm afraid that people who are determined to beat

the system are simply a fact of life," Ben said sadly. "But enough about Fish and Game's problems. Tell me about the project you've got underway."

"I'll let Laurel do that," said Dr. Wells. "In the meantime, I'm going to track down Trip." Frowning, he added, "I just don't understand him—"

"Dr. Wells is taking a biological inventory of Wolf Lake, studying its ecological structure," Laurel told Ben once they'd been left alone. "We're going to spend the next few weeks identifying every species of plant and animal that lives in and around it. Specifically, we're trying to find out why some lakes have rooted plants in them and others are dominated by phytoplankton."

She went on to describe the project in more detail. Ben Seeger was an attentive listener, stopping her every so often to ask a question.

When she finally finished, he said, "You sound as if you're pretty serious about all this."

"Oh, yes!" Laurel made no attempt to hide her enthusiasm. "I can't tell you how thrilled I am to be up here. It's always been my dream to come to a place like Alaska. Ever since I was a little girl, I've been in love with the natural world."

Ben chuckled. "If there's one thing we've got up here, it's nature." His expression suddenly became more serious. "Ever think of coming up permanently?"

"You mean to live?"

Ben nodded.

"I've still got three more years of college—"

"You mean you're this knowledgeable and you're only a freshman?"

Laurel was suddenly shy. "I'll be a sophomore in the fall."

"Tell you what. You give me a call in a couple more years, and if you're interested, I'll do what I can to set you up with a job as a field biologist. The Department of Fish and Game is always on the lookout for dedicated scientists like you."

Laurel could feel her cheeks turning red. "Do you mean it?"

Ben laughed. "Just as long as you don't mind a little mud, a little snow . . . and a few mosquitoes!"

"Mr. Seeger," Laurel replied earnestly, "to be perfectly honest, all that sounds like heaven to me!"

chapter
eight

"Come on, you dumb shoelace—oh, no!"

Frustrated over her inability to pull the fraying lace of her hiking boot through the last tiny hole, Mariah gave one hard tug—and watched with dismay as it tore in two.

"*Now* what am I going to wear?" she moaned, even though there was no one else in the tiny cubicle that served as a bedroom for three.

She'd been in Alaska for more than a week and a half, yet still she found even the smallest, most commonplace task a struggle. Even finding the right clothes to wear was a challenge. The fact that she'd brought all the wrong things didn't help. Her casual outfits from the finest department stores and boutiques may have looked fashionable, but she was quickly discovering they simply weren't strong enough to stand up to the hardship conditions of the Alaskan wetlands. She'd actually found herself envying Laurel her sturdy hiking boots and soft flannel shirts. At the moment, she would have gladly traded her favorite cashmere sweater for a pair of thick socks.

Not that she'd admit it. Mariah would have gone barefoot before she'd ask Laurel for help.

At the moment, doing exactly that looked like a distinct possibility. With a broken shoelace, there was no way she'd be able to wear her hiking boots on today's foray into the fields that lay beyond the wooded area on Wolf Lake's eastern shore.

"Come on, Mariah!" she suddenly heard Cassie call impatiently from the doorway of the cabin. "Russ and I are leaving. Dr. Wells said you've got to come *now*."

Feeling panic rise inside her, Mariah looked around the room. Her hiking boots, now useless, lay on the floor in front of her. Pushed in one corner were her running shoes, still sopping wet from the day before. The only pair of shoes that was even a remote possibility for the rigorous day ahead was a pair of white canvas tennis shoes. After only a moment's hesitation, she grabbed them and began pulling them on.

She knew what the others thought of her. And while she tried to tell herself she didn't care, the truth of the matter was that she hated being an outsider. She could see how close Cassie and Laurel were—even though she was constantly irritated by the way Cassie was always tagging along after Laurel. The only thing that was worse, as far as Mariah was concerned, was the way she kept fawning over Trip. And as far as *he* was concerned, she would have preferred working alongside a bear to working with him. Russ, at least, seemed reasonable. But he tended to keep to himself. That left Mariah little choice but to do the same.

"We're leaving, Mariah," Cassie called again. "Goodbye."

Mariah jumped off the bed and dashed out of the cabin. She immediately saw that Cassie hadn't been exaggerating. She and Russ were already starting down the path toward the lake, laden with the equipment they'd need for the morning's foray. Tagging along after them was little Danny Torvold. Just as he had on many other mornings, he was begging to be taken along on the day's outing, speaking in a high-pitched whine that set Mariah's nerves on edge.

"Hey, wait up!" she called, starting after them.

"Tennis, anyone?"

She turned and saw Trip and Laurel at the side of the cabin, helping Dr. Wells pack up the cumbersome fish-nets called seines. The three of them were going to spend the morning at the lake collecting more fish samples, not far from the field she'd be surveying with Russ and Cassie. At first, she'd been glad she'd be getting a break from her two least-favorite members of the team. Yet as Trip's jeering voice pummeled her like a spray of stones, she realized she wasn't going to get off quite that easily.

"Sorry if my fashion statement doesn't happen to come up to your standards," she shot back, barely glancing in his direction.

"Hey, this isn't the tennis courts of Beverly Hills," he retorted. "In case you haven't noticed."

"Hey, you two," Dr. Wells interjected. But he left it at that. Mariah figured he'd probably come to accept their sparring as something he was simply going to have to put up with.

I hate it here! Mariah thought as she hurried down the path toward Cassie and Russ, who were waving good-bye to a disappointed Danny. She shut her eyes hard, not wanting the tears that were beginning to well up to fall. How am I ever going to make it through another four and a half weeks?

She decided to ignore the others, instead concentrating on the work. Not that she was looking forward to spending this beautiful morning slogging around in a flooded field of muck, marshes, and swampy grasses. Why everyone else up here seemed to relish endless days in the most primitive conditions, she couldn't begin to understand. But today, just like every other day since she'd gotten here, she'd simply have to grit her teeth and, somehow, try to muddle through.

Please, *please* don't let this be as difficult as those long days in the canoes, Cassie thought as she followed Russ through the woods and into a clearing.

Almost instantly her spirits lifted. This, at least, was a pleasant change from the dense growth of trees that had surrounded her for the ten days she'd been up here, ten days that felt like an eternity. An expansive field stretched out ahead of her, a flat plain with nothing growing on it but stubby grass and some scattered wildflowers. Their mission for today was to survey the area, trudging through and gathering samples of plants and insects while taking notes on the varieties of birds they spotted.

She knew no more about this type of terrain than she did about the lake. Still, she was content to follow Russ around, doing her best to keep out of Mariah's way.

"Okay," he said. "Let's start over there."

"Why there?" Mariah asked.

"Because it's the farthest point in the area we'll be covering today. We'll work our way back."

"Okay," Cassie said with a shrug. Throwing her butterfly net over her shoulder, she took a step in the direction Russ had indicated.

Instantly she felt her foot going down, down, down. . . .

"Quicksand!" she cried.

"It's not quicksand," Russ said calmly. "It's muskeg."

"Musk *what*?"

"Muskeg. It's nothing worse than wet, spongy ground."

Cassie took another step, this one more tentative. Her boot sank into the soft ground a good eight or ten inches. A pool of water immediately surrounded her foot. "It's sucking me under!" she insisted.

"Don't worry; you won't go through. It's just a layer of decaying vegetation over a marsh. But it's strong enough to hold you up."

"Great," Mariah muttered. "There go my tennis shoes."

"Why didn't you wear rubber boots?" Russ asked.

Mariah was tempted to explain. Instead, she simply shrugged. "Come on. Let's get going." She headed in the same direction Cassie had started out in, her feet making a sloshing sound with every step she took. Russ and Cassie gripped their gear more tightly, then followed.

"Wait a minute." Suddenly Russ stopped. "We'd better not go this way after all."

"What now?" demanded Mariah.

"Look up there."

Cassie's eyes traveled upward in the direction he was pointing.

"I don't see anything." She was squinting into the sun.

"See what's up in that tree?"

"You mean those birds?" asked Mariah.

"Exactly. They're terns."

"Now I see them!" Cassie exclaimed. The birds were too far away for her to get a good look, but even from her vantage point she could see their distinctive black-and-white coloring. "They're beautiful!"

"Very nice," Mariah said impatiently. "Now let's hurry up and get this over with." She hiked her backpack higher up on her shoulders and started off.

"I wouldn't recommend going this way," Russ cautioned.

"But it's the shortest route!"

"We'd be better off heading around that way, along that little pond over there."

"You've got to be kidding!" Mariah made no attempt to hide her exasperation. "We must have walked two miles so far. Do you really expect me to tack on another extra mile because of some stupid *birds*?"

"Terns are extremely territorial," Russ explained. "Look in that tree, over there. See that nest?"

"Don't tell me," Mariah muttered. "That's the launching pad for their missiles."

Ignoring her icy comment, he continued, "The adult terns will do anything to protect their nestlings."

"I'm with Russ," Cassie agreed. "It's true that this other route is a little bit out of our way. But if he thinks it's for the best—"

"Tell me I'm not really hearing this!" Mariah rolled her eyes. "Are you two *serious*? You're actually afraid of a few little birdies?"

Russ opened his mouth, as if to protest. But he snapped it shut as Mariah gave a defiant toss of her head, then marched off in the exact direction he'd just warned her about.

"Honestly," she was muttering. "Of all the silly things I've ever heard in my life. . . ."

"Should we follow her?" Cassie asked Russ, her voice a hoarse whisper.

"No. Stay back." Gently he placed his arm on hers. But his eyes remained fixed on Mariah.

"Come on, you two scaredy-cats," she called over her shoulder, not bothering to look back.

Cassie was standing completely still. She realized her heart was pounding like a jackhammer as she watched Mariah make her way across the field. She could sense Russ's tension as well. He stood beside her, frozen as he watched.

Already the birds were reacting to the intruder. Cassie could see them flitting from tree to tree, making unsettling screeching noises. A few began swooping across the sky, gradually getting closer and closer to Mariah.

She, meanwhile, didn't seem to notice.

"Ooooh, I'm so scared," she yelled back at Cassie and Russ, her tone sarcastic. "Don't hurt me, birdies. Keep away. I'll be out of here in a few minutes; I promise." She was already far into the area that Cassie had figured out was the territory the terns thought of as their own. "I'll be waiting for you two adventurers on the other side," she called mockingly.

"We've got to stop her," Cassie cried.

"No, let her go," declared Russ. "Maybe this will teach her a little respect for nature."

"But will they hurt her?"

"Ooh, look at the pretty birdies." Mariah was prancing through the field. She'd finally noticed the half-dozen birds flying overhead, getting closer and closer. "See? They just want to be friends. Here, birdie, birdie!"

And then she let out a scream. One of the terns had descended from the sky, pecking at her head as it sailed past her.

"Oh, no!" Cassie cried. "We've got to help her!"

"They won't hurt her," Russ assured Cassie. "But if we're lucky, they'll scare her a little."

A second tern had already zoomed in for an attack, grabbing hold of a strand of Mariah's hair in its beak. It only held on for a second before darting off, but the shrill cry Mariah let out cut through the deserted field like an alarm.

"Help me! Help!" she cried. The backpack had slid off her back onto the wet muskeg. Both her arms were folded over her head as she desperately attempted to defend herself against the beating wings of the birds. They had all zeroed in on her, taking turns at swooping past her, sometimes taking a peck at her scalp, other times simply making terrifying squawking sounds.

"Help! Help!" Mariah shrieked again and again. She sank to her knees, her arms still covering her head. Not only did the birds continue their assault, she also began sinking into the marshy ground.

"We've got to help her," Cassie cried. Rushing toward Mariah, she was frustrated by how slowly she was forced to travel. The muskeg greedily grabbed at her feet, sucking her in with every step she took. But as she glanced over her shoulder, she saw that Russ was standing with his arms folded. And while he was trying his hardest not to laugh, he wasn't having much luck.

"Maybe this will teach Princess Mariah a little humility!" he called.

Ignoring him, Cassie trudged onward. Up ahead she could see Mariah crouched down and attempting to keep her balance on unsteady ground that gave way to whatever limb she put down on it. The birds circled her head, swooping and pecking and shrieking, refusing to give up their attack.

When she reached Mariah, Cassie yelled and waved her arms. The presence of two intruders was apparently more intimidating than just one. The birds finally moved away, hovering low in the sky. Their screeching continued, but at least they'd retreated.

"Let's get out of here!" Cassie exclaimed. She reached for Mariah's arm and dragged her to her feet. Mariah's face was streaked with tears and her designer sweater was spotted with tern droppings. She was sobbing.

"Are you all right, Mariah?"

"It was horrible! Absolutely horrible!" Standing

straight, brushing off her clothes, Mariah shrieked, "And it was all your fault!"

"My fault? Why?"

"You and Russ!" Mariah accused. "You're the ones who picked this route. This whole stupid thing was your idea!"

"But Russ tried to warn you!" Cassie was incredulous.

"He never explained to me what those birds were capable of." Her hazel eyes had narrowed into slits. "He wanted this to happen! He *planned* it! Don't think I didn't see him standing over there, laughing. *Laughing!*"

"Mariah, he didn't—"

"Those disgusting birds could have pecked my eyes out. I could be *blind!*"

Russ suddenly appeared, having made his way over to the two girls as they struggled to get away from the birds. He was laughing as he attempted to take hold of Mariah's arm.

"Get away from me, you . . . you *beast!*" Mariah screeched. "This was all your fault!"

Russ simply looked amused. "I should have known better than to think you might actually recognize that you played a part in this."

"You—you should have told me!" Mariah sputtered. "You knew, and you didn't tell me!"

With a shrug, he said, "I tried."

"He did, Mariah," Cassie was quick to agree. "But you wouldn't listen. You—"

"Get away from me, both of you!" Mariah barked. She grabbed her backpack and pulled it on roughly. As she did, huge dollops of mud from the muskeg splattered all over her jeans and the back of her shirt.

Cassie gasped, horrified.

"I'll get you for this!" Mariah declared, pointing her finger at him.

Russ opened his mouth to protest his innocence. But before he had a chance, they all started at the distant sound of Laurel and Trip yelling.

"What happened? What's wrong?" Russ was already running toward the sound of their voices, doing his best to travel quickly despite the soft sucking action of the muskeg and the ungainliness of his rubber boots.

"Over here!" Trip yelled. Suddenly he emerged from behind the thick growth of trees that edged the field a few hundred yards away.

"Is someone hurt?" Cassie cried.

"Everyone's fine," Trip returned. "Just come over here, will you?"

By the time Cassie, Russ, and Mariah reached him, all three of them were splattered with mud. Cassie was gasping for breath, nearly overwhelmed by the exertion of trying to run through muskeg. But it wasn't her own discomfort she was thinking about. It was the distraught look on Trip's face.

Her heart immediately began to race. She'd never seen him look so upset. In fact, she could barely remember having seen such a stricken look on anyone's face before. He looked as if he might be sick.

"Wh-what is it?" she demanded, surprised when her voice came out as a hoarse whisper.

"Brace yourselves," he instructed. "Russ, maybe you'd better look first."

Cassie opened her mouth to ask about Laurel one more time when her friend appeared behind Trip.

"Maybe you shouldn't look at all," she said to Cassie. Her face had the same sick look as Trip's.

"Why don't you tell us what this is all about?"

Mariah said crisply. "If this turns out to be some kind of joke—"

"This is no joke," Trip cut in, his tone deadly serious. "Someone's killed a bear. Shot him dead. From the looks of it, it wasn't a hunter . . . and it was no accident." He swallowed hard. "If you ask me, the poachers have struck again."

chapter
nine

"Where's the bear?" Russ asked, heading over in their direction.

"It's a pretty grizzly sight—if you'll excuse the pun," said Trip. "Somebody did quite a job on that poor animal."

Cassie swallowed hard. The Torvolds' words were echoing through her head. The image of bear poaching was repulsive: someone going out of his way to hire planes expressly to herd bears, selling off parts of the poor animals' bodies simply to line his own pockets. . . .

"Maybe none of you should look," Laurel was saying. "Frankly, I wish I hadn't seen it."

"What happened exactly?" asked Russ. "How did you come across it in the first place?"

"Trip and I were looking for botanical specimens," Laurel explained, "when all of a sudden we smelled something odd. It was really bad, the odor of rotting flesh. We followed our noses until we found the . . . the. . . ."

"Let me take a look," Russ offered. "Mariah, Cassie, wait here."

"No. We're coming, too," Mariah insisted.

Cassie would have been perfectly happy to stay behind. Yet as the other four tramped off somberly, she couldn't bring herself to beg to be left out. Instead, she followed, doing her best to brace herself against whatever it was she was about to see.

As she stepped between two large trees, peering over the shoulders of the others standing in front of her, she wished she really had stayed back. Her stomach lurched and a wave of dizziness came over her with such force she had to grab hold of one of the tree trunks to keep from sinking to the ground. Swallowing hard, she looked away.

Even so, the horrible image of what she'd just seen stayed with her. The bear carcass, covered with willow branches, was already beginning to rot. A cloud of flies surrounded the body. The head had been cut off, along with all four paws. On its side was a huge wound, caked with dried blood. Its belly had been slit open. And Laurel's description of the smell as "odd" was a real understatement. The stench made Cassie nauseous.

"See?" said Russ, pointing to the spot on the bear's side. "That's where he was shot."

"Look how they cut him up." Mariah's voice was strained.

"No doubt the poachers helping themselves to the parts they could sell," Trip said dryly. "It's just like Torvold said. They killed the whole bear to get a few dollars for two or three of its parts."

"What do we do now?" Mariah asked.

"We have to report this," Russ insisted. "First we'll tell Dr. Wells, of course."

"'I'm sure he'll want to report it to his friend at the Department of Fish and Game, Ben Seeger," said Laurel. "I imagine the more we can tell them about what we saw, the better their chances of catching whoever's responsible." Averting her eyes from the horrible sight, Laurel added, "As hard as it is to accept, chances are the person who did this will never be caught."

* * *

"Oooh . . . I hate this stupid thing!"

Mariah let out a cry of impatience, throwing down the fish trap she'd been struggling with for a good five minutes, trying without the slightest bit of success to untie the knots in the long string dangling from one end. Her fingers ached from the effort. She stood at the edge of the lake, shaking out her hands and feeling anger rise up inside her.

It wasn't only the tight little knots that were responsible for her frustration. The entire day had left her feeling unsettled. First, the broken bootlace as she was rushing to get out on time. Then, lugging heavy equipment through that awful muskeg, her canvas sneakers becoming saturated with her very first step. Next came the humiliating and terrifying experience of being attacked by terns. And after topping off the morning by confronting one of the most horrible sights of her entire life, she then had to witness Laurel's taking advantage of having stumbled across that poor dead bear to look good in front of Dr. Wells.

"I'll take you to the spot, if you want," Laurel had offered, her voice ringing out much louder than the others. "I remember exactly where it was. . . ."

Angrily Mariah tugged at the string. Being stuck up here in Alaska for four and a half more weeks was bad enough but the presence of Laurel Adams made it even worse. Looking down, she saw that all she'd accomplished was making the tiny knots even tighter.

"I hate this whole stupid trip!" she cried, fighting back the tears welling up in her eyes.

"There's an easier way to do that."

Mariah whirled around, caught off guard by the sound of a voice. She'd assumed she was alone out here, a good hundred yards away from the cabin. In fact, she'd made a point of choosing an isolated spot as she attacked this particularly tedious task.

The last thing she wanted to do was look like a fool—in front of Dr. Wells, in front of Trip, and especially in front of Laurel. Yet here Laurel was, standing with her hands folded politely in front of her, wearing that annoying patient look that she wore so much of the time.

"What are you doing out here?" Mariah demanded. Automatically she tried to hide the fish trap with the disastrous string—the result of her own failure to follow Dr. Wells's detailed instructions. Yet as she stood in front of Laurel with a metal fish trap half-hidden behind her back, she realized she was fighting a losing battle.

"Actually, I was looking for Dr. Wells," said Laurel. "I was wondering if I could go with him when he told John Torvold about the bear we found."

"He's not here," Mariah snapped.

"So I see." Laurel's eyes had traveled downward, to the trap. "If I were you, I'd take a knife and cut those fraying strings off. You'd be better off tying on new ones. Here, let me take a look at that one."

"Oh, no, you don't." As she barked her words, Mariah pulled the fish trap away from Laurel. She was pleased to see that her icy tone had precisely the effect she'd been hoping for. Laurel took a step backward, the expression on her face one of surprise. "Maybe you have everybody else around here fooled," Mariah went on, "but you can't fool me."

Laurel simply stared for a few seconds, her green eyes wide. "I don't know what you're talking about," she finally said.

"Oh, sure, you're trying to come across as an expert at everything under the sun. Laurel Adams, scientist *extraordinaire*. Well, if you ask me, you don't know any more than the rest of us. You're just a goody two-shoes, taking advantage of every opportunity that comes along to make *me* look incompetent! Never in my entire life have I seen anybody work so hard to rack up brownie points!"

By now, Laurel's expression was one of total disbelief. "Mariah," she began, "I wasn't—"

"And another thing," Mariah continued, unable to resist spewing forth the tidal wave of angry words surging up inside her. "If you're trying to impress Trip, I'll tell you right now you're wasting your time."

"Trip?" Laurel's mouth dropped open. "Mariah, I never in a million years—"

"I've seen you showing off in front of him. Believe me, I know boys like Trip. The last thing in the world that turns them on is a Miss Know-It-All."

"Are you finished?" Laurel asked woodenly.

"I am," Mariah shot back. "I only wish you were."

Her expression stricken, Laurel turned. Glancing over her shoulder, she called back, "By the way, whenever you untie fish traps out in the field, make sure you undo the knots on the spot instead of just pulling them off the clumps of grass. That way, you won't get stuck with a dirty job like that." She turned away, vanishing into the woods.

Mariah stood with her arms folded across her chest, watching Laurel disappear into the woods. She was certain she'd got her point across, putting Laurel in her place once and for all. Yet there was one thing that left her completely confused. And that was why having done so didn't make her feel one bit better.

Laurel hurried into the cabin, wanting nothing more than to be alone. Inside she was raging. She was furious at herself for letting Mariah get the best of her.

How *dare* she accuse me of showing off . . . especially in front of Dr. Wells! she thought, closing her eyes tightly to keep from crying. It was true that she was anxious to impress him. But she was sincerely interested in this project—not only in learning as much as she could, but also in being a valuable contributor to his research.

Yet in trying her hardest, was she really coming across as a brownnose, a teacher's pet . . . a goody two-shoes?

Suddenly Laurel was awash in confusion. So many different feelings were rushing through her. Anger at Mariah, disappointment in herself . . . and, of course, the bad feelings that continued to lurk at the back of her mind, her dismay over her parents' reluctance to accept her love of science.

When she spotted a letter lying on her bunk, she was instantly heartened. She hadn't even been aware that any mail had been delivered. Eagerly she grabbed the envelope, hoping it would turn out to be good news.

Then she read the return address. The letter was from her mother. She hesitated before slitting open the cream-colored envelope, expensive-looking writing paper she now realized she should have recognized immediately as her mother's. Her fingers were tense as she unfolded the piece of thick paper inside.

"Dear Laurel," she read. "It's so hard for me to imagine you so far away, in that wild place unlike anywhere I've ever been or even conceived of going. . . ."

Laurel braced herself. Part of her wondered why she was even bothering to read on, since the tone of the letter's introduction made it clear where it was going.

"I wish I could be more supportive, dear," her mother had written in her crisp, neat handwriting, "but I'm still not certain you're heading in the right direction. The road you've chosen to travel is such a hard one. It's especially difficult for a girl. . . ."

Suddenly Laurel found being inside the cabin confining. Still clutching the letter, she raced outside, hurrying down the path and into the woods. She didn't stop until she'd reached a huge cottonwood tree at the edge of a small clearing. Sitting cross-legged on the soft ground, leaning against the trunk, she read through the rest of the letter.

"I know you've never been one to follow the pack, Laurel," it said. "Even as a little girl, you were always off on your own, ignoring everyone else as you chased after butterflies or spent hours studying a spiderweb. You were never interested in the things the other girls were interested in.

"I hoped you'd grow out of it. I did my best to get you involved in more traditional pursuits. Remember your sixteenth birthday party? I made a point of inviting your entire private school class hoping I could help you fit in better.

"And now this. My heart breaks over the image of you living in a tent somewhere, dressed in sloppy clothes, spending long days hiking or paddling around in a canoe. A girl your age should be out having fun—"

"But it *is* fun!" Laurel cried aloud, talking to someone who was, in reality, five thousand miles away. "It's *my* idea of fun, Mother! Can't you understand that? Can't you accept that?"

But the only answer was the lonely cry of a loon off on the lake, the hollow sound eerie as it cut through the still air.

chapter
ten

"Bad news, Laurel?"

Laurel glanced up from the letter she'd been forcing herself to read, resisting the temptation to crumple it into a ball and throw it away. She saw Russ standing in front of her, his face tense with concern. Hastily she blinked away the tears in her eyes.

"I didn't mean to disturb you," he said earnestly. "I called your name, but you didn't seem to hear."

"That's okay."

Russ gestured toward the letter with his chin. "I hope nothing's wrong."

"No, not really." She folded up the cream-colored paper and stuck it into the pocket of her jeans. "Just a letter from home."

His frown deepened. "Are you sure everything's all right?"

"Yes, everything's fine." With a high-pitched laugh, she added, "At least, as fine as it ever is."

"I don't understand."

"It's a long story." Laurel waved her hand in the air dismissively. "One that's too boring to go into right now." Peering at him more closely, she noticed he was standing in an odd position, with one hand stuck behind his back. "Are you hiding something, Russ?"

"Well, not *hiding* it exactly . . . More like waiting for

just the right moment." His cheeks were flushed as he took his hand out from behind his back. He came out with a small, colorful bouquet of wildflowers. "These are for you."

"For me?"

Russ nodded. He kept his eyes down, acting as if the moss-covered rocks dotting the forest floor were something he'd never seen before. "I-I came upon a whole clump of them just now and. . . . Well, I'd overheard your argument with Mariah and I figured you could probably use some cheering up." Awkwardly he thrust the bouquet of deep purple lupine interspersed with bright pink fireweed at her.

"Oh, Russ. They're lovely. Thank you so much." Laurel hesitated only a moment before reaching for them. A peculiar thought flitted through her head: why on earth was Russ giving her flowers? The first response that came to mind was simply too absurd to contemplate. Quickly she dismissed it.

He already told me, she insisted to herself. He overheard what Mariah said to me and thought I might be in need of some cheering up. . . .

"Russ," she asked suddenly, putting the flowers aside, "do you think that since we've come up here, I've been acting . . . like a show-off? Trying to impress everybody with how much biology I know?

"Not that I think I know that much," she added hastily. "I mean, compared to you, for example, I'm practically a beginner. But the last thing I want to do is give the impression that I think I'm better than everybody else—"

"Oh, no!" Russ was quick to assure her. "Not at all! As a matter of fact, I've been really impressed by how much you know."

Laurel smiled wanly. "Thanks, Russ. That means a lot to me."

"There is one thing, though. . . ."

She looked at him expectantly.

"Every once in a while when I find myself watching you, I can't help noticing that you seem kind of . . . pre-occupied."

Laurel found herself growing uncomfortable. Russ . . . watching her? Why? That admission, added to the bouquet of wildflowers he'd so bashfully presented to her, made her original suspicion impossible to ignore. So he really did have a crush on her.

She decided to pretend not to notice. Instead, she would simply treat him like a friend.

"As a matter of fact," she said, "I have been a little preoccupied. And this letter is part of what I've been wrestling with." She sighed. "I'm afraid my parents aren't very supportive of my decision to pursue a career in science."

"You're kidding."

"I wish I were."

"Why aren't they?"

Laurel laughed coldly. "My mother thinks it's not very ladylike."

"You mean somebody actually feels that way in this day and age?"

"Yes! Mother would much rather I'd spent the summer shopping for a husband—someone respectable, with a promising future, someone who'd take care of me for the rest of my life—rather than running around Alaska, collecting damselflies and poring over the Peterson field guide, identifying wildflowers."

Russ was pensive for what seemed a very long time. "You know, Laurel," he finally said, "it sounds as if the family I grew up in was as different from yours as night is from day. My parents were kind of rebellious. They both left their families to live in virtual isolation on a nature preserve. I grew up pretty much the same way Danny Torvold is.

"All that presented problems of its own . . . like the fact that now that I'm grown up, I never feel as comfortable being around a lot of people as everybody else seems to. I've always been pretty much a loner. Not that I mind, but, well, every once in a while I find myself wishing I were a little bit more like everybody else. You know how it is—kids getting together and talking about the TV shows they watched when they were growing up, the trips their family took to Disney World. . . .

"But the bottom line is that I wouldn't trade my upbringing for anything. Maybe I didn't have a lot of the same experiences and material things as other kids my age. But there's one thing my parents gave me that's much more valuable than any of that: the sense that I have to be the kind of person *I* want to be. When you grow up pretty much cut off from the rest of the world, the way I did, you tend to see things in much simpler terms. And that includes sorting through everybody else's expectations of who and what you should be and coming up with a clear idea of what it is *you* want.

"That's a struggle I think everybody faces as part of growing up. And it's one I think I've pretty much been able to bypass, thanks to my parents' values and the fact that I've always had to look inside for answers, rather than having the option of looking outward."

He laughed self-consciously. "I didn't mean to make a speech."

"I appreciate your honesty," Laurel said sincerely. "You've been very helpful."

Blinking, he said, "I have?"

"Yes. You're absolutely right. I do have to keep clear sight of what I want. This is my life, not anyone else's. And I guess it doesn't hurt to be reminded of that every once in a while."

She reached over and placed her hand on his shoulder, giving it a squeeze. "Thanks, Russ."

His face turned bright red. "Well, uh, I'm glad I could be of assistance."

Laurel smiled. "You have." She ran her fingers lightly over the soft petals of the colorful flowers. "Knowing I have a friend is more of a help than you know."

Cooking out the following Saturday night was Dr. Wells's idea, his way of acknowledging that his research team was doing a good job—and that they deserved a break. Late that afternoon, he asked for volunteers to take the van and make a run into town for supplies.

"I'll go!" Cassie piped up before anyone else had a chance. "And Laurel will come with me. Oh, please, Laurel!"

Laurel had to admit it was a welcome change of pace, driving the van along the bumpy dirt road. Beside her in the front seat, her copilot chirped away happily.

"I can't wait to see civilization again!" Cassie cried, resting her feet on the dashboard. "Imagine, I'm actually getting excited over the prospect of walking into a supermarket! That just goes to show you what a couple of weeks in the middle of nowhere can do to a person."

Laurel smiled. "If I didn't know better, I might think you sounded as if you were actually having fun up here."

"I wouldn't go that far. But maybe I am getting used to it, at least a little." With a shrug, Cassie added, "Still,

I'm enjoying a trip back into the real world. Driving to the store like this almost feels like home."

Suddenly Laurel slammed on the brakes. A porcupine had just lumbered across the dirt road, less than twenty feet in front of the car. Cassie and Laurel looked at each other, then broke into hysterical laughter.

"Well," said Cassie, "*almost* like home."

For Laurel, stepping into a modern supermarket after two solid weeks surrounded by nothing but trees was a shock. As for Cassie, she darted around happily, racing down every aisle, thoughtfully considering each end-aisle display.

"Oreos!" she cried, grabbing two packages off the shelf. "I'd practically forgotten they existed! How have I ever managed to live so long without them?"

"Take it easy," Laurel warned, laughing. "We're only supposed to buy food for tonight's cookout, remember? Don't get carried away."

"I have to stock up," Cassie insisted. "After all, who knows how long it'll be before I see an entire mountain of cookies again?" She'd already pounced upon the Chips Ahoy.

It turned out she wasn't the only one who'd missed the amenities of the civilized world.

"Is that really Coca-Cola?" Trip greeted the two girls as they strolled into the cabin laden with grocery bags. "Or am I dreaming?"

"It's real," Cassie assured him.

"Hey, I don't suppose you picked up any tortilla chips, did you?"

Cassie looked crestfallen. "Gee, Trip, if I'd known there was anything special you wanted, I'd have been happy to pick it up for you."

"There was no point in going to any trouble—"

"Oh, no!" she was quick to assure him. "It wouldn't have been any trouble at all."

Mariah, curled up on the couch, cast a knowing glance in Laurel's direction. She, in turn, simply looked away.

Junk food aside, Laurel had to admit it was fun, building a big fire in a clearing and roasting hot dogs on the open flame. Sitting cross-legged on the cool ground, downing her third hot dog and washing it down with a can of Cassie's precious Coke, she realized that the five of them, not to mention Dr. Wells, had spent nearly every waking minute working ever since they'd arrived. Sitting back and simply relaxing was a treat.

"This is more fun than I'd expected," she observed.

Her comment had been directed at Russ, who was sitting next to her. But Mariah leaned forward, daintily dabbing at her lips with a paper napkin.

"The word 'fun' doesn't begin to describe it," she observed dryly. "This is just like camp. All that's missing is an arts-and-crafts counselor, forcing us to make birdhouses out of ice-cream sticks."

"Maybe we should sing," Trip suggested. In a fake, high-pitched voice, he sang, "Kum-ba-ya, m'Lord—"

"I have a better idea," Mariah interrupted.

In the flickering light of the campfire, Laurel could see her hazel eyes gleaming. Something about the peculiar expression on Mariah's face made Laurel very uncomfortable.

"Let's play a game."

"How about strip poker?" Trip's face lit up.

"Actually," Mariah said, "the game I had in mind is much more intellectual. Not to mention one that'll help us all get to know each other a little better."

Laurel glanced over at Cassie. Her friend looked as nervous as she felt.

"The game is called Truth."

Russ shook his head. "Never heard of it."

"It's easy to learn," Mariah insisted. "One of us makes a statement, and the others have to guess whether it's true or false."

"I still think strip poker sounds like more fun," Trip said, popping a roasted marshmallow into his mouth.

"Trust me. This game can be *lots* of fun. I'll start." Mariah glanced around the small circle. "Okay, here's my statement. One of the girls in our group has a burning crush on one of the boys, and one of the boys has a crush on one of the girls."

"Are you talking about the same girl and the same boy?" asked Laurel.

"No." Mariah smiled wickedly. "That's the fun of it. What do you think, Cassie? Is that statement true or false?"

"I-I really have no idea," Cassie sputtered, her eyes fixed on the flames of the fire, just beginning to die down.

"I'll take that as a pass. How about you, Russ?"

"I pass." He picked up a stick and, reaching over, used it to stoke the fire.

"Come on, you guys," Mariah said impatiently. "Don't you know how to have fun?"

"I'll answer," Trip volunteered. "I'd say the statement is true. Now we can all spend the next four weeks wondering who the mystery players are in your little soap opera.

"Now it's my turn. Ready?" He paused dramatically before making his statement. "One of the girls in our group is extremely jealous of one of the other girls here. Mariah?"

"I . . . you . . . the . . ." she sputtered. It took her a

few moments to regain her composure. "I'd say that's completely false!"

"Ah, Mariah," Trip said, shaking his head, "you're taking all this too personally. You're simply assuming that I'm talking about you. You're taking all the fun out of the game!"

"I gave my answer," she replied crisply. "I said your statement was false."

"Well, it happens to be true."

"How do you know it's true?" Mariah challenged.

"Come on, you two," Laurel interrupted. "I don't know if this game is supposed to be fun, but it's not. Let's find something else to do—or better yet, let's start cleaning up."

"No, wait," Cassie said boldly. "I have one."

"It's not your turn," Mariah insisted.

"It's still my turn, since you didn't get it right," said Trip, "and I gladly relinquish it to the lovely Cassie."

"Thanks, Trip." Her eyes lingered on him for a moment, a shy smile on her lips. "Okay. Here goes. There's a person here who's determined to ruin the entire summer for the rest of us. Anybody want to take a stab at that one?"

"I'll make that a definite pass," said Russ.

"Me, too," Laurel agreed quickly.

"It's Mariah's turn, anyway," said Trip. "She got the last one wrong."

"That statement is false," Mariah said tartly.

"Considering that playing this game was your idea in the first place," Trip interjected, "you're not turning out to be very good at it."

"Maybe you were right." Mariah rose to her feet. "This game isn't turning out to be as much fun as I'd thought."

"Is that it?" Trip demanded, his voice harsh. "Or is it that the truth is simply too hard for you to take?"

"I'm outta here." Mariah was already heading into the woods, toward the cabin.

"Hey, aren't you going to help clean up?" Cassie called after her.

But she was already gone.

"Here's a statement," Cassie muttered. "There's one very lazy person in this group."

"I don't think Mariah's lazy," Laurel said. "She was just upset."

"Ah, Laurel," said Trip, slinging his arm around her shoulders. "You're so sweet. So innocent. Always giving everybody the benefit of the doubt—"

"Not everybody." Firmly she removed his arm.

"You're terrific, Laurel. Our own little peacemaker. How would we ever manage without you?" Laughing loudly, he wandered off toward the lake.

Laurel frowned. "Great. The two of them take off, leaving us to do the cleaning up—"

"I don't mind," Russ insisted. "I'd rather do all the work than have Trip and Mariah hanging around, making our lives more difficult." He sighed. "And we've still got four weeks left. Four *long* weeks." Shaking his head, he began picking up plates.

Laurel bent down to help him clean up. She instantly became absorbed in retrieving bits of paper from the ground. It wasn't until she stood up, her hands full, that she noticed that her best friend was standing a few feet away, simply staring at her. And the look in Cassie's eyes was anything but friendly.

chapter
eleven

Over the next few days, Laurel tried to convince herself she was simply imagining Cassie's coldness. With the team breaking up into pairs every day, she and Russ working together at Dr. Wells's suggestion, she saw little of her during the day. In the evening, when Cassie and her partner, Mariah, returned, they were all too busy working independently for there to be much interaction. By the time they finished with the day's work and retreated to their bedrooms, Laurel, like everyone else, was too exhausted to talk.

So she was particularly looking forward to the group's next foray out into the field together. She hoped that working side by side with Cassie once again would give her a chance to get a reading on her mood.

"Today I'd like you to take the canoes out to that little island at the far end of the lake," Dr. Wells told them early one morning at the end of the third week. They were gathered outside the cabin, near a decaying wooden picnic table that often served as a makeshift lab in the evenings. "You know what to do when you get out there: use the fish traps and the seines to get fish samples, use the sweep nets to collects insects, gather botanical specimens . . . and I think it's time we started setting animal traps."

"Oh, no!" Cassie cried. "That's so mean!"

"There's nothing mean about these." Like a salesman launching into a demonstration, Dr. Wells reached under the table and pulled out a big boxlike contraption, setting it on the picnic table.

"Have-a-heart traps," said Russ.

"Have a *what*?" asked Mariah.

"These are live traps," said Dr. Wells. "That means they trap animals without killing them."

"We'll let them go afterward, right?" Cassie asked anxiously.

"We certainly will. All we want to do is find out what's living in the woods surrounding the lake—and the island in the middle of it. Here, I'll show you how the traps work. First, you put a mixture of peanut butter and rolled oats on the trigger, like this. Then you find a sheltered place in the brush to put the trap. After you've left the area, sooner or later some small animal will happen by and jump at the chance for a free lunch. The next thing he knows, he's inside this cage . . . and we've got our specimen to study."

"What do you expect to find around here?" asked Trip.

"Marmots, tree-climbing squirrels, maybe a snowshoe hare—"

"This is so exciting!" Laurel said. "I can't wait to get a close look at all those different types of animals."

"The downside of these traps," Dr. Wells went on, "is that every once in a while you get an animal who becomes trap happy. He learns he can get food simply by spending the night in a trap. Once he figures out what a good deal that is, he might spring the trap before other animals are caught."

"The secret is to keep the traps moving," said Russ. "Instead of setting them in the same area day after day, pick out different areas."

"I'll start loading them into the canoes," Laurel offered. She picked one up and started heading down to the lake, the others following not far behind.

The routine of packing up the canoes was familiar by now. Expertly Laurel loaded in the trap along with all the usual gear. There were also provisions for the day. Today would be a particularly long day, since the island was close to two miles away. They'd brought along enough food to keep all five of them fortified for a good twelve hours.

"This canoe's all set," Laurel finally said. Smiling, she turned to Cassie. "Are you ready?"

Her smile faded when she noticed how Cassie stiffened.

"No thanks, Laurel. Russ and I have already agreed to go together today."

"Oh. Okay." Laurel blinked in confusion. "How about you, Mariah? Want to share?"

"I'm always a willing partner," Trip offered.

"Oh, no," Mariah protested. "If you two pair off, that makes me odd one out. There's no way I'm going out in one of those things alone. I'll go with Laurel."

As she stepped into her boat and Trip into his, Laurel noticed that Cassie had a smug look on her face.

It was another perfect day, the lemon-colored sun slowly making its way across the southern sky, cloudless and a soft shade of grayish blue. For some time now Laurel had been thinking of this place as home. She felt she belonged here. When she was out on the water, she felt united with her magnificent surroundings. She was swathed in a sense of peace unlike any she could remember having experienced before.

They had pushed off from shore and begun paddling across the lake when Trip called, "Hey, Laurel. I've got a proposition for you."

Behind her, Mariah muttered, "What now?"

"A proposition?" She was instantly suspicious. "What kind of proposition?"

"Let's agree to call a truce for today."

Laurel's eyebrows shot up. Glancing over her shoulder, she said, "I hadn't realized we were in the midst of a battle."

"I'm only trying to make it easier—"

"Okay, okay. You're right. And I think it's a wonderful idea. For the sake of science—not to mention group harmony—today we'll play it straight. You'll promise not to come on to me—"

"And you'll promise to treat me like a colleague, rather than a party boy."

Laurel laughed. "It's a deal."

They had just reached the island when Trip came up to her. "I need a partner for seining. What do you say?"

"Sure," she replied with a shrug.

"I'll get in the water, since I've got the footwear for it. Even with those rubber shoes of yours, you'll be much better off staying on shore."

She took hold of the brown handle he handed her, one end of the heavy fish net that reminded her of the net from a tennis court. Seines were difficult to use. Because they were so large and heavy, dragging them through shallow water to catch small fish was hard work. Still, using one enabled the team to get specimens too small to be caught in the fish traps and to collect fish of all sizes on the spot rather than waiting a day or two to catch them in the traps.

"So tell me," Trip said as they pulled the net through the water, struggling to move as quickly as possible without tripping over a submerged branch. "How did a girl like you first get interested in the wonderful world of creepy crawly things?"

"To tell you the truth, I can't remember a time when I *wasn't* interested in the natural world," Laurel replied sincerely. "Even when I was really little and all the other girls were playing hopscotch at the playground, I'd be wandering around the grass, looking for interesting bugs."

"I bet that made you popular," Trip said sarcastically.

"You're right. No one could understand why I wasn't into the same things as everybody else. Least of all my parents. My mother is a great believer in—"

She never did finish her sentence. All of a sudden, something large and unyielding pushed against her. The ground beneath her feet was rocky and uneven, and she was so close to the water's edge. . . . Before Laurel understood what was happening, she was knee-deep in lake water.

"I'm *so* sorry!" someone behind her cried.

Leaping out of the water and back onto the shore, Laurel turned around angrily.

"You pushed me in!" she accused Cassie, who was standing a few feet away, holding a sweep net.

"I did not!" Cassie returned. "It was an accident— honest! I saw this really cool-looking butterfly, and I started running after it—"

"It didn't look like much of an accident to me," Trip commented. From the mischievous grin on his face, it was impossible for Laurel to tell whether he was telling the truth—or trying to stir up a little trouble, just for his own enjoyment.

"Great," Laurel grumbled. "Now I'm going to have to walk around with wet feet all day—"

"I didn't do it on purpose!" Cassie insisted.

"It was so careless of you—"

"Maybe if you'd been paying attention to what you

were doing, instead of telling Trip the story of your
life. . . ."

Cassie's angry words affected Laurel more strongly
than the sensation of sopping wet socks over cold,
damp feet. She simply stared.

"It wasn't my fault," Cassie insisted. "And if you
think I'm going to go around feeling guilty all day,
you're wrong."

Sticking her chin up in the air, she said, "Now if
you'll excuse me, I have important work to do."

"What's *her* problem?" Trip muttered after she'd
stalked off.

Laurel let out a deep sigh. "I wish I knew."

Trip picked up her end of the seine and handed it to
her. "Come on, Laurel. We've got important work to
do, too."

She gazed after her friend only a moment longer before taking the end of the net and once again taking her
place by the edge of the lake.

After coming in from the long day on the lake, Cassie made a beeline for the tool shed, where the single
metal shower stall used by all six members of the research team, as well as the Torvolds, was housed. She'd
hoped the hot water would melt away some of her bad
feelings. Yet as she towel dried her headful of red curls,
she was aware that there was as much tightness in her
neck and shoulders as there'd been all day.

She came back to her room, hoping this would turn
out to be one of the rare times she actually managed to
be by herself. But it was only minutes before Laurel
wandered in, standing awkwardly in the doorway as if
she were waiting for something. Cassie pretended to be
absorbed in folding the clothes she'd worn that day.

"You certainly seemed to have fun today," she finally said, her tone crisp.

"Yes, it was fun," Laurel replied. "At least, after my feet dried off."

Cassie kept her eyes down. "I told you, Laurel. It was an *accident*!"

"Cassie, what's going on with you?" Laurel demanded.

"Nothing. I'm absolutely fine."

"You don't seem fine."

Suddenly Cassie whirled around. "Just leave me alone, will you?"

Laurel took a few steps backward. The expression on her face was one of complete surprise—and confusion. But Cassie barely took the time to look. She was too busy rushing out the cabin, desperate to get away. As she dashed toward the door, she noticed her backpack on the couch. Suspecting she'd want to stay away for a long time, she grabbed it.

How *could* she! Cassie was thinking as she raced down the stairs, into the woods. I saw what she was doing. Making a play for Trip, flirting with him all over the place. . . . How could she be so insensitive? I never in a million years thought my best friend would go out of her way to steal a boy away from me! And accusing me of having pushed her into the lake on purpose, right in front of him. . . .

Her heart ached so badly it felt as if it would burn right through her chest. She ran and ran, taking care not to trip over the gnarled roots of trees or to get her foot caught in the clumps of tall grasses. She nearly slipped on a rock, but caught hold of the low-hanging branch of a tree just in time. By now, the tears were flowing freely down her cheeks. *How could she?*

Never before had Cassie felt so strongly about a boy.

Sure, she'd had her share of crushes. And she'd had a few boyfriends along the way—nothing serious, but certainly enough to keep her from feeling as if she were missing out on the romantic scene most of the other girls in her high school had been so involved in. In college, she had yet to find anyone special. There'd been a few movie dates, quite a few long conversations over coffee at the Student Center, an intense two-week infatuation with her first-semester English professor. . . .

But nothing like this. These feelings, the way her heart fluttered whenever she even thought about Trip, were new. Cassie found it impossible to let more than a few minutes go by without thinking about him. She felt as if they were linked somehow, in some deep, spiritual way that made them destined to be together. It had to be love. It had to be the real thing.

Of course, Trip had yet to make any acknowledgment of their connection. As a matter of fact, Cassie thought morosely as she stopped at the edge of the lake to catch her breath, he barely seemed to notice that she existed. But that was why it was so important that the two of them have time—time, without any distractions. Distractions like Laurel. If only Trip had the chance to get to know me, Cassie told herself. If only he'd step back and see me for what I really am.

She sank to the ground, taking deep breaths to calm herself down. As she did, she noticed how beautiful it was out here by the lake. She realized she'd been so wrapped up in getting through her busy days that she hadn't been taking enough time to notice.

Suddenly she caught sight of a clump of water lilies, bobbing lazily in the lake a few yards ahead. Curious, she got up and wandered over to get a better look.

Resting on top of the lake, amidst large, flat, circular leaves, were huge yellow blossoms, so colorful and so perfectly formed that they barely looked real. Their petals curved upward to create a ball. Cassie had never seen such a dramatic flower.

Before she'd even realized what she was doing, she'd unzipped her backpack and was scrounging around for a pad of paper and a drawing pencil. It was only the third or fourth time she'd had a chance to draw since she'd gotten to Alaska. She settled in comfortably on the bank, choosing an angle at which the sun illuminated the flowers in just the right way. Without wasting a single moment, she bent her head over the pad and began to sketch.

As she did, her ruminations about Trip and Laurel and even herself faded away. The only thing that existed was the display of exotic flowers Mother Nature had so generously laid out before her. She was completely absorbed in getting the curve of this line just right, capturing the exact way in which that shadow sloped over the leaf and then changed its angle when it hit the rough surface of the lake.

Cassie finally became aware that somewhere along the line, her neck had begun to ache. But the tightness in her muscles was different than before. This time it was from physical strain—not emotional. She stretched, meanwhile looking around. She had no sense of how much time had passed. It could have been ten minutes—or it could have been two hours. She simply didn't know.

In fact, at that moment there were only two things she felt completely certain of. One was that she'd drawn a detailed black-and-white sketch of the water lilies that truly captured their beauty, bringing them to life on the flat white page with almost as much drama as they possessed in real life.

The other was that she felt totally refreshed. Her

mind had been cleared in a way that could only come about by having created something. Standing up, noting that the stiffness of her muscles indicated she'd been working for quite a long time, Cassie realized that the different parts of her life were suddenly in much better perspective.

She was still angry at Laurel. And her heart ached when she thought about Trip and the pointed way he'd ignored her all day. Yet, at the same time, she understood that there were other elements in her life as well. She had drawing and painting, which she loved more than anything else. And that, no one could ever take away from her.

She flipped over the page of her sketchbook, while looking around with a critical eye. Her gaze finally lit upon a clump of wildflowers. The purple lupine stood proud and strong, their delicate petals forming a graceful silhouette. Picking up her pencil, she started to draw.

It wasn't until Cassie felt someone tap her lightly on her shoulder that she realized she wasn't alone. She turned around abruptly and found Dr. Wells standing behind her.

"Oh, hello, Dr. Wells," she said breathlessly. "I didn't hear you—"

"Sorry. I didn't mean to startle you." He stooped down and peered over her shoulder. "What have you got there?"

"Oh, nothing." Quickly Cassie pulled her sketch pad up to her chest. She could feel her cheeks turning red.

"If it's nothing," Dr. Wells asked, his expression one of amusement, "then why are you being so secretive?"

"Well . . . they're just drawings."

"Drawings?"

"Just some sketches I've done up here. Flowers,

mostly. A few of animals." Shyly, she added, "I don't know if they're any good or not."

"Would you mind if I took a look?"

Cassie hesitated. She didn't want to show them to anybody ... especially Dr. Wells. Still, she didn't see how she could turn him down without looking silly.

Without a word she handed him her sketch pad. She stared off into the distance as he turned the pages, pretending to be lost in a daydream. She told herself she didn't care what he thought. Still, her heart was pounding.

He'll probably hand it back to me with a polite, "Very nice," she told herself.

So she was surprised to hear him say, "My goodness, Cassie, I had no idea you were such an accomplished artist!"

She looked over at him, astonished.

"Your father mentioned you were interested in drawing and painting," he continued, "but he never let on that you were so talented."

"Thank you," she mumbled. Then, anxious to break the silence that followed as he went back to the beginning of the sketchbook for a second look at some of the earlier drawings she'd done, she added, "I'm certainly getting enough inspiration. So many of the plants and flowers are unusual varieties, unlike anything I've ever seen before.

"Of course, I haven't done a lot of drawings of plants. I've pretty much stuck to the still lifes you get stuck doing in art classes. Or landscapes. I've tried my hand at those a few times. I'd like to tackle some animals while I'm up here. As you can see, I've tried a few drawings of birds, but it's hard because they never stay still for very long."

"Yes," Dr. Wells said slowly, handing her sketch pad

back to her, "I think you should do birds. The plants, as well. And everything else you come across.

"As a matter of fact," he said, looking her straight in the eye, "I'd like to assign you a special task."

"What's that?"

"I'd like you to provide documentation of the flora and fauna of this ecosystem."

Cassie just blinked.

In response to her apparent confusion, Dr. Wells laughed. "What I mean is, we're here to describe the plants and animals living around Wolf Lake. But our findings will be much more meaningful if we can back them up with detailed drawings."

"What about photographs? Wouldn't they be better?"

"Photos have important uses, of course. But they simply can't capture structural detail as well as drawings. Here, look at this one." He pointed to the last picture he'd studied, the drawing of the clump of lupine. "See how you've drawn these fine lines to show the vein pattern on the leaves here? It would be difficult for a camera to pick up such fine detail. That's particularly true when you're looking at something with a lot of color—like the dark green surface of this leaf—since color can overwhelm anatomical detail."

"I see what you mean," Cassie said, nodding.

"So how about it? May I start considering you the project's official artist?"

"I'd love it," she blurted out.

"Good," Dr. Wells said with a smile. "Consider it done. What I'd like you to do is make drawings of particular specimens I point out to you, but also to take it upon yourself to go around the lake, doing these careful detailed pictures of whatever catches your fancy. If something looks interesting and unusual to you, chances are that it's something worth taking a closer look at. Does that sound acceptable to you?"

Cassie just nodded. She didn't want to let on that for the first time since she'd found out she was going to be part of this research project, she finally felt as if she belonged.

chapter
twelve

"Where are you going today?" Danny Torvold asked anxiously, skipping alongside Trip, Laurel, and Russ as they trudged from the cabin down to the lake. They were all laden with equipment and provisions for the day's outing. Russ was carrying a particularly cumbersome load, a huge telescope that was balanced across one shoulder. Trying to be helpful, the nine-year-old boy insisted on holding one of the fish traps. It banged against his leg with each step he took down the rugged dirt path.

"Out on the lake, my man," Trip replied. "Where else is there?"

"Can I come, Trip?" Danny pleaded. "I won't be any trouble, I promise. Maybe I could even help! I know my way around this lake better than anybody else—except my mom and dad, of course. I could show you some really cool places—"

"Not today, pal." Trip barely glanced at Danny. Instead, he focused on loading the fish traps he'd been juggling into one of the canoes. "Want to give me a hand over here, Russ?"

With dismay, Laurel noticed that the boy looked crestfallen. She was about to offer him some consoling words. But before she had a chance, Russ spoke up.

"Tell you what, Danny," he said cheerfully. "I know

we've already been up here for a while, but I bet there are still some ins and outs we have yet to discover on our own. How about giving me my own personal guided tour of this lake? I'm sure an expert like you could show me some great things."

Danny brightened immediately. "You got yourself a deal! I'm ready any time you are."

"How about tonight, after we get back?"

"Sure! Catch you later!"

Danny dashed off. Instead of the forlorn expression he'd been wearing only moments before, he looked as if he'd just been given a wonderful present.

"You certainly have a way with children," Laurel commented, setting down the armful of equipment she'd hauled to the lake's edge.

Nestling the day's lunch in the back of one of the canoes, Russ shrugged. "I was just like him, once. Living on a preserve, alone most of the time. . . . Besides, it's good for any kid to be made to feel important. Everybody knows that."

"Not everybody," Laurel commented, casting a meaningful look at Trip.

A moment later Cassie came hurrying down the path.

"Sorry I'm late," she said. Her apology was directed at Trip.

"No problem," he replied. "Her Majesty has yet to put in an appearance, anyway."

By the time Mariah appeared—a good ten minutes after the time the group had planned to get going—the canoes were packed and everyone was ready to go.

"That girl has an uncanny sense of timing," Trip muttered. "The second we finish all the dirty work, she makes her grand entrance."

Glancing up, Cassie's expression changed to one of

astonishment. "Where does she think she's going?" she demanded. "A photo shoot?"

As Mariah grew closer, Laurel saw what she was talking about. Not only was Mariah dressed in an outfit that looked as if it had come off the pages of a fashion magazine, but she was wearing quite a bit of jewelry. In addition to a pair of gold earrings, glinting in the sunlight, she sported a long, dangling necklace and a thick gold cuff bracelet.

"I didn't know formal attire was required for today," Trip commented.

"Maybe you're content to dress like somebody who was raised by wolves," Mariah shot back. "But some of us like to feel human every once in a while."

"At least she's here," Russ said pointedly. "Now we can get started."

"Who's going with whom?" asked Laurel.

Russ shrugged. "I'll take Mariah."

Trip leaned over, a smirk on his face. "Better you than me, pal."

"Cassie?" said Laurel. "Want to share a canoe?"

Cassie shrugged. With an air of complete indifference, she said, "Fine."

"I guess that makes me the odd one out," said Trip.

"You mean you're just figuring that out *now*?" Mariah commented dryly.

Once the three canoes had left the shore and were drifting purposefully across the glassy surface of the water, Mariah asked, "So what are we doing today?"

"I thought Dr. Wells's briefing last night made that pretty clear," replied Russ.

"I was too tired to listen. Something about animals, wasn't it?"

Russ shook his head slowly, as if he couldn't quite believe what he was hearing. "We've got to check the live traps and the fish traps from yesterday. And we've really got to work on identifying the species of birds living around Wolf Lake."

"I get it. That explains why you're lugging that big telescope out into the wilds. And here I thought you were just getting nearsighted in your old age."

"It's called a spotting scope, and it's the best thing for observing bird behavior. As soon as I find a good place to set it up—" Russ suddenly stopped. "Hey, look at that red-throated grebe!"

"Fascinating," Mariah muttered. "Just fascinating."

After that, she had little to say. A few hours later, as the group paddled into one of the deeper parts of the lake to collect aquatic insects with long-handled dip nets, Laurel realized she'd barely said a word all morning. In fact, Mariah rarely interacted with the others— not only today, but every day. Yet instead of resenting her, Laurel actually found herself feeling sorry for Mariah. In a strange way, Mariah reminded her of Jim Whitehorse. Both of them lived in a kind of isolation— quite different in most ways, to be sure, but not completely without similarity. She wondered why Mariah was so difficult to get along with . . . and why she was so difficult to get to know.

After a while, her mind wandered away from the other girl's odd behavior back to the beauty of the lake. Just like all the other times she'd been out on the lake, it was hard not to become completely absorbed by it. She let all other concerns drift out of her head as she allowed herself to be hypnotized by the rich colors, the sweet air, and the musical sounds that completely surrounded her. As far as she was concerned, she'd be happy to stay out here on the lake forever. It was so peaceful, so idyllic. . . .

"My bracelet!" Mariah suddenly cried, her voice shrill.

Startled, Laurel glanced over in her direction. She saw the stricken look on Mariah's face.

"It's gone! My bracelet's gone! It must have fallen into the lake!"

"Lesson number two hundred seventy-three," Trip muttered. "Never wear jewelry from Tiffany's, Cartier, or other exclusive, overpriced Beverly Hills boutiques while paddling a canoe—"

"You don't understand. That's not just any bracelet. It was—I have to get it back."

Russ was about to voice his protest when Mariah suddenly jumped to her feet, leaning over the side of their canoe and peering into the water below.

"Look out!" he yelped.

It was too late. The canoe tipped over, sliding effortlessly over the smooth surface of the lake and turning over one hundred eighty degrees. Russ and Mariah were thrown into the lake, along with the nets, the day's provisions, the logbook, the telescope, and all the other gear that had been stashed inside for the day's research trip.

Mariah sat in the lake, water up to her chin, the tops of her knees barely breaking the surface of the lake. The expression on her face was one of total astonishment.

"The equipment!" Laurel exclaimed, horrified.

"*And* our lunch," muttered Cassie.

"Good going, Mariah," Trip said under his breath.

Russ was the angriest of all. He'd fallen into the lake right along with Mariah. Standing knee-deep in water, he gasped, "Of all the thoughtless things you've ever done—"

"It's not here!" Mariah gasped. "I still don't see my bracelet!"

Trip shook his head. "Boy, are you hopeless."

Mariah attempted to stand, her eyes still fixed on the bottom of the lake. But as she struggled to find firm footing, she let out a whoop and slid right back into the water. She plunged down even harder this time, her head slipping beneath the surface of the water. When she finally managed to pull herself up, she was coughing and spitting out lake water. Her wet hair hung over her head like a shiny black veil.

"Somebody—get—me—out—of—here!" she sputtered.

Russ stuck out his hand. "Just promise me one thing, Mariah," he said from between clenched teeth. "From now on, whenever we go out on the lake—"

The shriek Mariah suddenly let out kept him from finishing.

"Get them off! Get them *off*!"

It took only a split second for Laurel and the others to understand what had happened. Mariah's slender arm, once sporting a stylish gold bracelet, was now covered with black squiggles.

"Leeches!" Cassie cried, her eyes wide.

"Oh, Mariah." Laurel was transfixed by the repulsive sight.

Trip was less sympathetic. "Oh, for heaven's sake. A few leeches never hurt anybody."

"Get them off me!" Mariah's voice was shrill with panic. Her face had crumpled into a look of total despair.

Russ grabbed her arm and began methodically picking off the slimy black shapes. Laurel couldn't tell whether the scowl on his face was due to his disgust over having to deal with the bloodsucking worms . . . or Mariah's hysteria.

"Look!" Mariah suddenly exclaimed. "I'm bleeding!"

"That's what happens when you pull off a leech," Russ explained calmly. "It leaves behind a calling card."

He had almost finished when Mariah cried, "I just thought of something. More of those . . . those horrible *things* could be attaching themselves to my legs as we're standing here in this horrible lake! Let's get out of here *now*!"

Russ glanced around. They were fairly far from shore. But the small island they'd explored days before was only a hundred yards away. "That island's our best bet."

"Help me onto it—*please*!"

"Why don't you climb into our canoe?" Laurel offered.

"Oh, no you don't," Cassie insisted. "The last thing I want is for her to topple ours, too. Thanks, but an armful of leeches is not my idea of a good time."

Mariah was sobbing as she crawled onto the rocky shore on her hands and knees. When she was finally on firm footing, she sank to the ground. Anxiously she examined her legs. When she saw nothing out of the ordinary, she buried her face in her hands.

"That was horrible!" she sobbed. "And my bracelet's lost forever!"

"Losing our lunch was horrible," Trip muttered. "Dr. Wells wants us out on the lake until eight or nine tonight. By that time, we'll all have starved to death."

"We don't have to starve." Cassie had been silent for some time, and the sound of her voice was a surprise.

"All our food fell into the lake," Russ reminded her.

"I brought along some of my own." She unzipped her backpack and began rummaging through it. Her cheeks were pink as she held out her stash of candy bars, cookies, and chips. "It's not much ... but it's better than nothing."

"All right!" Trip had already pounced upon a bag of chips. "Cassie, I love you!"

Her cheeks grew even redder. "Anybody else want something?" She gestured toward the pile of snacks.

"I'll take this for later." Laurel helped herself to a candy bar. "Thanks, Cassie. You really saved the day."

"Great," said Mariah. "Here we are trapped on Gilligan's Island, and all we've got to eat is junk food. Chocolate, potato chips. . . . Do you have any idea how many grams of fat are in those?"

"Gee, Cassie," Trip said, his voice dripping with sarcasm, "the next time Mariah throws all our food into the lake, make sure you pack a well-balanced meal. Salad, tofu, a few bean sprouts—"

"I'll scout around the island," Russ offered. "Maybe I can find some wild berries."

"Make sure they're organically grown!" Trip called after him.

As Russ wandered into the wooded area further inland, Trip turned to the girls. "Look, we've still got a long day ahead of us. As soon as Russ gets back, we should get back into the canoes and head further out on the lake."

"Who put you in charge?" Mariah challenged.

"Mariah," Laurel said evenly, "we've got a job to do. Just because you're a little wet—"

"I wonder how you'd feel if you'd just fallen into a lake and gotten covered with leeches!"

"Laurel's too smart to stand up in a canoe," countered Trip.

"Maybe you should take one of the canoes and head back to the cabin, Mariah," Cassie suggested. "I'm sure the rest of us could manage—"

"Trip! Laurel!" From inside the wooded area came the sound of Russ's voice. And it was filled with alarm.

When he emerged from the woods, the expression on his face matched his tone.

"What is it?" demanded Trip.

Russ took a moment to catch his breath. "I think I've just found another casualty."

"What are you talking about?" Mariah asked crossly. And then she froze. "Not another bear."

"I'm afraid so." Trip's face was drawn into an earnest expression. "Anybody care to take a look?"

"I will," Laurel said bravely.

"Me, too," said Trip. He'd already headed toward the woods.

Following the two boys, Laurel braced herself for what she knew she was about to see. Sure enough, on the other side of a dense growth of bushes lay a large dark mass. This carcass was in the same shape as the other one. Someone had shot a bear, cut off parts of it, and left it to rot after covering it with willow branches. The smell was also the same. Even though she'd known what to expect, she grabbed hold of a tree branch to keep herself from getting dizzy.

Trip stood over the dead animal, shaking his head in disgust. "Just like the other one."

"Let's be careful not to touch anything," said Laurel. "We've got to tell Dr. Wells."

"And we've got to tell Fish and Game," Russ insisted.

"Hey, look over here!" All of a sudden, from somewhere behind them, Cassie's excited voice cut through the woods.

"What now?" Trip muttered.

"Come see what I found!" Cassie called once again.

Laurel went first, with the boys close behind. She found Cassie a few yards away.

"What is it?" asked Russ.

"Look at this." Cassie was pointing to something bright red, hanging from a tree.

At first Laurel thought it was a flower. But as she looked more closely, she saw it was a scrap of fabric. Her heart began to pound.

"Maybe this tore off the poacher's clothes!" said Cassie.

Mariah, who was standing closest to the tree, reached up as if she were going to take it down.

"Don't touch it!" Russ warned. "Cassie's right. This could be an important clue."

"Let me see that." Laurel leaned forward to study the scrap more closely. It was a piece of coarse wool, red fabric edged with black. "This looks like it's from one of those hunters' jackets. You know the type: red-plaid wool, with black lines that form a checkered design."

"I know exactly the kind you're talking about," Trip agreed. He paused, a meaningful look on his face as he glanced around at the other members of the group. "And isn't it a coincidence that somebody who lives around here happens to own one."

chapter
thirteen

The group was silent for a long time.

When Cassie finally spoke, her voice was thin and uncertain. "We can't be positive this piece of fabric is from Jim Whitehorse's jacket. Laurel said it herself. A lot of hunters wear that type. Campers, too, and fishermen and hikers. . . . There must be thousands of people in the state of Alaska who own jackets like that."

"Yes, but only one of them lives around here," Trip insisted. "If you ask me, it doesn't take much to put two and two together."

"Careful, Trip," Russ warned. "Cassie's right. Let's not start jumping to conclusions. We'll tell Dr. Wells about what we found, and he'll report it to Ben Seeger. Aside from that," he added, shrugging his shoulders, "there's nothing more we can do."

Later that evening, the five of them were quiet as they sat in the living room. The somber air hovering over them was made even more oppressive by the heavy rain that had begun to fall. It hammered at the roof relentlessly, bringing with it dark, forbidding skies.

"Who wants to deal?" Cassie asked, the cheerfulness in her voice strangely out of place in this atmosphere. She sat at the table, shuffling a deck of cards.

"Not cards," Mariah groaned.

"Do you have a better idea?" Russ glanced up from

the table, where he was sitting opposite Cassie, leafing through Peterson's field guide to the birds of North America.

Trip, standing in front of the open refrigerator, called over his shoulder, "How about the Truth game?"

Before Mariah had a chance to react, Laurel broke in. "I don't know about the rest of you, but I can't concentrate on anything until I find out what Ben Seeger has to say."

"Dr. Wells should be back any minute," Russ pointed out.

Laurel glanced at her watch impatiently. "He's been at the Torvolds' forever. How long does it take to telephone Anchorage?"

As if on cue, just then Dr. Wells strode into the cabin. The expression on his face told them instantly he didn't have anything encouraging to report.

"I reached Ben at home," he told them. "And he was pretty upset. Unfortunately, he wasn't very reassuring. He said the same thing as last time, that the Department of Fish and Game simply doesn't have the resources to investigate every incident of bear poaching as fully as it might."

"Great," said Trip. "So he'll write up a report that gets stuffed in a drawer with a hundred other pieces of paper—and does nothing more than gather dust."

When Dr. Wells left, Cassie turned her attention back to her cards. "Okay, who's in? Your choice of Rummy Five Hundred, Go Fish, Crazy Eights—"

"We have to do something." Laurel was pacing up and down the room restlessly, like a tiger confined in a cage.

"That's why I suggested cards," said Cassie. "Otherwise we might all die of boredom."

"I'm not talking about cards. I'm talking about the bears."

"Give it up, Laurel." Mariah, nestled in one corner of the couch, pulled her long black hair over one shoulder. Distractedly she began stroking it.

"Mariah's right," Cassie agreed. "If the entire Alaska Department of Fish and Game can't catch the poachers, why on earth would you think—?"

"Just because Ben Seeger's not particularly optimistic doesn't mean there isn't some way of getting to the bottom of this. Maybe if we all put our heads together. . . ." Pleadingly Laurel looked around at the other four.

"Count me out." Trip sank onto the couch, the last can of Coke in his hand. "I came up here to further science, not to play Sherlock Holmes."

"Mariah?" asked Laurel. "What about you?"

Mariah raised one eyebrow. "You're joking, right?"

"Cassie?"

Cassie didn't even look up from the cards she was slapping on the table, dealing them out into two piles. "Sorry, Laurel. Just seeing those poor dead bears was bad enough. I have no desire to go roaming around in the woods, looking for clues—or whatever it is you have in mind."

"But Cassie! We—"

"I'll help," Russ offered with a little shrug.

"Somehow I had a feeling you might volunteer," Mariah said dryly, a knowing look on her face.

Laurel simply ignored her. "That's great, Russ. Thanks. Now all we have to do is come up with a plan. . . ."

Before any of them had a chance to respond, a familiar voice rang out through the rhythmic pounding of the rain.

"Anybody home? Is it okay if I come in?"

Danny Torvold appeared in the doorway, his face flushed with excitement. His hair was drenched, the dark red strands hanging down straight, forming fringe around his freckled face.

"Hi, Russ!" he exclaimed. "Hi, everybody."

"Hey, Danny," Russ called back. "What are you doing out on a terrible night like this?"

"I didn't want you to think I was backing out on our deal."

Russ shook his head, clearly confused.

"I promised I'd take you out on the lake tonight, remember? I figured you'd probably realize it was raining too hard, but I wanted to make sure you didn't think I forgot."

"To tell you the truth, I'd got so wrapped up in other things that I'm the one who forgot."

"Oh, yeah. The bears." Danny's expression grew serious. "My mom and dad were really upset when they heard. Me, too."

"We're all upset," Laurel said gently. "In fact, we were just talking about whether or not it made sense for us to do a little investigating of our own."

"You mean try to find out who's been killing the bears by yourselves?" Danny's eyes had grown wide.

"Exactly," said Laurel.

"Gee," Danny said eagerly. "I'd sure love to help!"

"Great," Trip muttered. "Not only do we have a crackerjack team of two gung ho college students on the case, but now we have a nine-year-old boy, too."

Laurel cast him the dirtiest look she could manage. But before she had a chance to put her two cents in, Russ spoke.

"In the first place," he said slowly, "as Danny himself told us, he knows the area around the lake better than anybody. I felt the same way about the preserve in

New Hampshire where I grew up. In the second place, we have two things the Department of Fish and Game lacks."

"Oh, really?" Trip asked cynically. "And what, may I ask, are those?"

"Time . . . and commitment."

Trip snorted. "Time? I don't know about you, but if there's one thing I don't have, it's time. As for commitment, my first commitment is to this project. I'm here to help Dr. Wells, not to play hero."

"Who knows?" Russ said with a shrug. "Maybe we'll be able to do both."

Mariah closed her eyes and leaned her head back against the soft couch, trying to ignore the conversation going on around her. At that moment, she would have given anything for a long, hot bubble bath. . . .

"Everything okay?" Cassie asked. Despite her sympathetic words, there was little kindness in her voice.

"Everything's fine," Mariah insisted. "I'm just tired, that's all."

"Sure you're tired," Trip joked, "after today's little—"

"That's enough, Trip."

Surprised, Mariah glanced over at Laurel. She was the last person in the world she'd ever have expected to come rushing to her defense. Her outrage over being put in a position where somebody else pitied her, combined with her dismay over the events of the day, suddenly overwhelmed her.

"I'm going to bed," she said stiffly, standing up and stalking into the bedroom.

It wasn't until she was alone, curled up on her cot with the covers pulled over her head, that Mariah allowed the tears to fall. She sobbed quietly, burying her face in a wad of tissues. The last thing she wanted was for any of the others to hear.

Mariah saw crying as an act of weakness, and she felt completely foolish. Yet she couldn't help it. And the disdain of the others played only a small part in her feelings of desperation.

The gold bracelet that had fallen into the lake had been her mother's, one of the few things she'd owned that Mariah still had. Her father, nearly destroyed by her unexpected death at the hands of a drunk driver, had been so distraught that he'd given practically everything else away. The bracelet, his present to her on their twenty-year wedding anniversary, only three days before the car accident, was something he'd been unable to part with.

Dr. Burke had given it to Mariah the day before she got on a plane in Los Angeles to fly east to begin college.

"Here, Mariah," he'd said, his voice gruff. He stood awkwardly in the doorway of her bedroom, unable to look her in the eye as he handed her a small bundle wrapped in white tissue paper. "Your mother would have wanted you to have this. And since you're going off to start a brand-new life for yourself tomorrow, this seems like the perfect time."

She'd cherished that bracelet. She hadn't worn it all year, afraid something might happen to it. When it was time to pack for Alaska, she'd hesitated only a moment before sticking it in her bag. It occurred to her that bringing it along might ward off some of her apprehensions about the summer ahead.

The only reason she'd dared put it on that morning was that she'd been feeling so miserable. So completely alone. Maybe, she figured, having something of her mother's with her would help. . . .

And now it was gone. Mariah closed her eyes. She was tired from the long day; even more, she felt drained.

She could feel sleep coming on, and she welcomed it. As she began to drift off, she counted how many days of the research trip still remained. There were three weeks left. At the moment, that sounded like a very long time ... so long, in fact, she wondered how she was ever going to make it.

"Dr. Wells was very understanding about us wanting to take some time for ourselves this morning," Laurel commented.

Thoughtfully she dipped her paddle into the lake water. It was an action she'd carried out hundreds, maybe thousands of times before. Yet she couldn't help noticing how different being out on the water felt today, compared to all the other days.

This morning, she was on a mission. Laurel, Russ, and Danny had started out first thing, promising Dr. Wells they'd be back in a few hours. All three of them were anxious to start scouting around the area, trying to uncover some clue, some piece of evidence, that would help them figure out the identity of the bear poachers. An air of apprehension hung over them, rooted in the knowledge that they were not out on the lake in the name of science, but in an attempt to investigate a horrible crime.

"I think our best bet," said Russ, "is to start out where we found the second bear. Let's head over to the island."

Danny brightened. "I've been playing on that island ever since I was three years old!"

"Good," said Laurel. "Then you should be able to spot anything that's unusual."

The three of them were subdued as they made their

way across the island, stepping carefully over fallen logs and densely overgrown patches as they headed toward the spot they'd discovered the day before. Danny had no problem keeping up with them; in fact, he seemed quite at home. Still, while he kept his eyes open, desperately wanting to help Russ and Laurel by identifying something about the island that looked different, he found nothing.

"This is where we found the bear," Laurel finally said, her voice hushed. She'd paused a few feet before the spot, grabbing hold of a tree branch to steady herself.

"Let me see," Danny insisted.

She cast Russ an anxious look. "Are you sure you want to, Danny?"

"Maybe I'll see something you missed."

In silence the three of them pushed through the heavy spruce branches. Even though Laurel had tried to prepare herself for the gruesome sight, she drew her breath in sharply. Glancing over at Danny, she saw that all the color had drained from his face.

"I sure hope you find out who's responsible for this," the boy said simply.

She placed her hand on his shoulder but said nothing.

"Here's that piece of fabric." Russ had gone over to the bush a few yards away from the bear. "It's wet from last night's rain."

Laurel frowned. "Maybe we'd better take it with us. The longer it's out here, the more tattered it'll become . . . and the less useful it'll be."

"Let me see that." Danny reached for the scrap. "I recognize this. It's from a jacket that belongs to Mr. Whitehorse."

"Danny," Laurel said gently, "just because Mr.

Whitehorse has a jacket that looks kind of like this doesn't mean this came from it."

"It sure looks like the same kind of material." Danny glanced up at her. "Do you think he did it?"

"At this point, I don't know what to think. We're still at a stage when we simply need to find out as much as we can."

Danny hesitated, fingering the damp fabric. "I have an idea. I could take you to where he lives. Maybe . . . maybe you'd find some clues there."

Automatically Laurel glanced at Russ. "What do you think?"

He was thoughtful for a few seconds. "I think we'd better."

"Okay." Laurel's stomach had knotted up. All of a sudden, she'd been hit by the grim reality of what she and Russ were trying to do.

Jim Whitehorse's cabin was impossible to reach except by canoe. After paddling to the farthest end of the lake, Laurel and Russ trudged after Danny for close to twenty minutes before he finally gestured with his chin.

"This is it," he told them, stopping at the edge of a clearing. "It looks pretty quiet. I have a feeling he's out in the woods somewhere."

The building was a simple structure. It was small, probably nothing more than one room. By comparison, the log cabin in which Laurel and the others had been living was luxurious.

She'd been curious about the quiet loner ever since she'd gotten to Alaska. But now that she was a few feet away from the place in which he lived, she felt uneasy.

"I-I don't think we should be here," she told Russ. "I feel like we're spying."

"We're trying to find out everything we can, that's

all," Russ reminded her. "We're not doing anything we shouldn't be doing." He studied the cabin. "I'm going to get a closer look."

"Russ, are you sure—?"

"Stay here." He'd already taken off, leaving Laurel behind with Danny.

"Come on, Danny," she suggested. "Let's walk around out here. Maybe you'll notice something out of the ordinary."

Russ reappeared a minute or two later, shaking his head as he approached. "I looked through one of the windows, but I couldn't see very much. It's kind of dark in there. And from what I could see, it's just the stuff you'd expect to find: a few pieces of furniture, some books, a little kitchen area."

"We haven't had any luck, either," said Laurel. "Danny and I have been looking around here in the woods."

"There is one thing I *did* find. . . ." said Russ.

"What?" Laurel and Danny asked in unison.

"The most fascinating spider I've ever seen in my life. Danny, I was wondering if you might be able to help me identify it."

"Sure thing!" Gleefully Danny skipped away after Russ.

Laurel smiled. She decided to leave the two of them alone. She wandered off, keeping her eyes open for something—anything—that might prove helpful.

She walked behind the clearing in which the cabin was centered. Back there the woods were thick and hard to cross. She found herself holding onto branches to keep her balance. Sharp twigs scratched her arms and legs. When one of them scraped her face, she let out a little cry.

She was thinking about turning back and finding Russ and Danny when she suddenly got the feeling that someone was watching her. There was nothing tangible to give her that idea—not a noise, not anything she'd seen—just the eerie sensation that she wasn't alone.

Instinctively she whirled around. "Russ? Danny?" she called, peering through the woods, struggling to see. "Is anybody out here?"

But there was no response except the chirping of birds and the rustle of leaves.

A chill ran down Laurel's spine. You're imagining things, she told herself. It's just the wind. Or maybe some animal, stealing through the underbrush. . . .

Instead of going back, she forced herself to walk on. She walked more slowly, taking care not to make any noise. Her heart was pounding so loudly she was certain it was echoing through the forest.

And then, after passing through a particularly dense growth of trees, she found herself in the midst of a clearing. The pounding of her heart was louder than ever. She blinked hard, not certain she was really seeing what she thought she was seeing. Yet there was no mistaking it.

There, in the midst of the clearing, parked a few hundred yards behind Jim Whitehorse's cabin, was a plane.

"It was the exact same kind of plane John Torvold told us the poachers generally use," Laurel said breathlessly. "A supercub, one of the PA-18s with those big tundra tires."

"We have to be careful," Russ warned. "A lot of people in Alaska own planes." Thoughtfully, he added, "They're very common . . . just like red plaid jackets."

He pushed aside the mosquito netting and gestured for her to go into the cabin ahead of him. Just as she'd hoped, the others were still out. After the three of them paddled back to the cabin, Danny had gone back to his own house, leaving Russ and Laurel alone to talk.

"It's so hard not to jump to conclusions." She sank onto the couch. "We don't have a lot of evidence . . . but so far everything we do have seems to point to the same conclusion: Jim Whitehorse is responsible for the bear poaching."

"Maybe it'd be helpful if we talk to someone at Fish and Game about it," Russ suggested, sitting down at the table. "They might be able to give us some insights."

"Good idea. Let's talk to Ben Seeger the first chance we get. In the meantime, we should probably keep a careful record of all the clues we come across. I have an extra spiral notebook I brought along. Let's keep a log, writing down what we do and when we do it."

She headed into her bedroom to get the notebook. She was lost in thought, trying to make sense of all that was unfolding. It was so hard to imagine the possibility that someone who lived right here at Wolf Lake—someone who the Torvolds knew, who the Torvolds *trusted*—could be involved in something so despicable. . . .

Suddenly she stopped. Lying on the floor in front of the bunk beds was a white envelope. Written on the front in a large, almost childish scrawl, were the words, "To the blond-haired girl."

"What on *earth* . . . ?" Laurel's voice trailed off as she bent down to pick up the envelope. She held it for a few seconds, examining the peculiar handwriting. As she did, a strange, sick feeling rose up inside her. Slowly, with trembling fingers, she opened the envelope.

Inside there was a single slip of white paper. It was unusually thick, unlike any she'd ever seen before. One edge was jagged, the sharp irregular triangles a sign that it had been ripped out of some kind of book.

On it, in the same unusual handwriting that had been on the envelope, were written four simple words: *"Keep out of it!"*

chapter
fourteen

Laurel's heart was pounding as she walked into the living room and handed the note to Russ.

"Read this," she said, her voice a hoarse whisper.

He glanced at the note, the muscles of his face tensing. When he looked up at Laurel, he was flushed. "Who do you think sent it?"

"There's only one person who could have." She swallowed hard. "Jim Whitehorse."

Shaking her head slowly, Laurel sank into the chair opposite Russ. "He must have seen us prowling around his cabin this morning. I didn't say anything about this before, but when you and Danny were looking at that spider and I was walking around by myself, I got the feeling somebody was watching me. I thought it might have just been my imagination, but. . . ."

"It all adds up," Russ said, nodding. "Somebody wants to keep us from discovering who's responsible for the bear poaching—and that somebody appears to be Jim Whitehorse."

"We'll have to tell Dr. Wells about this note," said Laurel, studying it. In here, the light was much better. She saw it had been written with a very fine pen, one that made a very narrow line with breaks here and there. "Maybe all three of us should talk to Ben Seeger about the fact that it looks like Jim Whitehorse is our man."

Russ frowned. "There's one problem."

"What's that?"

"We don't have any proof. So far, all we've got are a few pieces of circumstantial evidence. A swatch of fabric that matches Jim Whitehorse's jacket—and a few hundred other people's jackets, as well. The fact that he owns the kind of plane a lot of bear poachers use. And now a note—a note we have no way of tracing to him."

Laurel sighed. "You're right. We're still making assumptions, aren't we? Jumping to conclusions we have no right to make—"

"Conclusions about what?" Trip had just come striding into the cabin, wearing a big grin. "What'd I miss?"

"Oh, nothing," Laurel replied quickly. "We were just . . . gossiping."

"How did your little expedition go this morning?" asked Mariah, coming in right behind Trip. "Catch any bad guys?"

"Actually, it was rather uneventful," Russ returned with forced heartiness. "You were probably right to keep out of it. Playing private investigator is turning out to be nothing but an exercise in frustration."

"Hate to say I told you so, but. . . ." Mariah had already lost interest. She'd gone over to the refrigerator and was poking around inside. "Anybody have any ideas about lunch? I'm starved."

Trip bounded over to the kitchen. "That leftover sandwich from last night is mine. Keep your hands off it."

Laurel took advantage of her moment alone with Russ to lean over and ask in a quiet voice, "What now?"

"We need to find out more," Russ replied. "Let's give it some time."

"What's up for today?" Cassie asked over breakfast the next morning. "Fish, bugs, or birds?"

"I've decided to make today a holiday." Dr. Wells set his coffee mug down on the table. "You deserve a break. Why don't the five of you take the Jeep and go somewhere? There are some spectacular glaciers just north of here, with valleys that are great for hiking. Or you could drive to the coast and check out some of the tiny villages there. The churches are particularly interesting. They were put up by the Russians who were the first to settle this area—"

"How about renting a room at the local Holiday Inn?" Mariah suggested. "Imagine, a steaming shower in a luxurious bathroom. A heated swimming pool. Room service. Now that's my idea of a break."

Dr. Wells laughed. "No such thing, I'm afraid. That's not exactly Alaska's style."

"I'm with Mariah," said Cassie. "I crave civilization. I'd like nothing better than the chance to spend the day in the company of other human beings. Poking around shops, walking on a real sidewalk . . . maybe even eating in a restaurant." With a sigh, she added, "I'd give anything for real, live french fries!"

"The closest thing to what you're describing is the town of Homer, nicknamed 'the end of the road,' " said Dr. Wells. "Not exactly a booming metropolitan area, but I suspect you can find french fries there."

"In that case, I make a motion we head into Homer."

Mariah raised her hand into the air. "I second the motion."

The two boys responded with a grimace.

"Uh, oh," said Cassie. "Two to two."

"Laurel, it looks like you're the tiebreaker," said Dr. Wells, chuckling. "What's it going to be?"

She looked around at the others, blinking. "How can you compare eating french fries with the chance to see an actual *glacier* . . .?"

Cassie and Mariah groaned.

Still, everyone's spirits were high as the five of them set off for Byron Glacier in the Jeep. Trip insisted on driving. Laurel sat next to him in front. Russ, Mariah, and Cassie were crammed into the backseat. Stashed in back was all the gear they'd need for their all-day hike: maps, a camera, food, water . . . and a big bottle of sun block.

"How's the shoe situation back there?" Trip asked, looking at Mariah through the rearview mirror.

"Fine, thank you," she replied evenly. "Fortunately, L. L. Bean even ships to Alaska." She raised her foot upward, showing off her new tan suede hiking boot.

"Hey, look out!" Cassie cried. But she was laughing as she pushed Mariah's foot away, shoving Russ even further into the corner. "This isn't a fashion show!"

"I want to prove to Trip that Beverly Hills girls aren't completely lacking in common sense," Mariah teased.

"Or credit cards," Trip shot back.

This is *fun*, Laurel reflected, glancing around at the others, all of them laughing together like the best of friends. For the first time since she'd come to Alaska, she actually felt as if she were part of a team.

The drive up the coast to Byron Glacier was nothing short of spectacular. On one side of a narrow two-lane highway the turquoise Kenai River rushed south toward Cook Inlet. Salmon fishermen stood shoulder to shoulder, their fishing poles clutched in their hands. On the other side of the road, glaciers in high mountain valleys hung above rounded slopes.

They headed along the shore of Turnagain Arm, a tremendous inlet cut into the mountains by glaciers millions of years ago. In the distance, far beyond the glassy water, were snowy mountains, their white tops blending into the thick white clouds that hovered above making it impossible to see where the mountains ended and the sky began.

Every mile or so, Trip pulled the Jeep over to the side of the road so everyone could scramble out and get a better look. Along the beach, Laurel and Cassie collected interesting rocks. Russ and Trip had a race up a pile of ominous-looking boulders that had tumbled down from the mountains during an avalanche aeons earlier. By the time they actually reached Byron Glacier, they'd already put in a solid half day of sightseeing. Yet, instead of being tired, they were exhilarated over the prospect of a long, challenging hike.

They parked in a small lot at the edge of the park that surrounded Byron Glacier. There were fewer than a dozen other cars parked there, mostly vans and campers. After packing up and pulling on their backpacks, the five of them started up the dirt path that cut through the dense woods and into a valley.

A few hundred yards beyond was a view so breathtaking that Laurel let out a gasp. Triangles of white snow zigzagged across black mountains, rising up dramatically on either side. The valley in between was a mixture of green and fields of snow. Down the middle was strewn a path of dark, angular boulders, most of them huge. Meandering through was a stream, its white water tumultuous.

"Look at the snow!" Laurel exclaimed.

"Look at those boulders!" Cassie cried. "How are we ever going to get across this valley?"

"Easy," Trip returned. "It's called rock hopping." To

demonstrate, he scrambled onto one of the rocks, almost as big as he was, then leapt onto the one next to it. "Piece o' cake."

Cassie wasn't convinced. "It looks dangerous."

"I'll walk right behind you," Laurel offered.

"That's okay," Cassie said quickly. "I'll manage."

Laurel felt as if she'd been slapped. Here she'd been thinking things were going so well, that the members of the group were finally getting along ... and that the tension she'd felt between Cassie and her could well have been nothing more than her own tendency to be overly sensitive. Yet the prickliness in Cassie's tone was unmistakable.

Rock hopping turned out to be more strenuous than Laurel had anticipated. Conversation came almost to a halt as the group made its way across the valley: Laurel and Trip in the lead, Russ following, Mariah and Cassie lagging behind. The three in front stopped every now and then to give the other two a chance to catch up.

"Are you two managing okay?" Russ asked congenially.

"I'm glad I had my Wheaties today," Mariah puffed. "Otherwise I'd tell you to leave me on one of the rocks to contemplate the melting snow while the rest of you went ahead."

But even she claimed it was worth it when the group finally made it to Byron Glacier. Laurel paused on one of the rocks, taking a moment to catch her breath and take in the incredible view. The glacier was a luminescent shade of blue-white. What struck her even more than the beauty of the color, however, was its monumental size. It cut through the mountains, easily as formidable a presence as the highest peak. Gazing at it, she had a sense of how it had plowed across the forbidding terrain through the ages, taking on even the tremendous mountains that in the end proved no match for its determination.

"Wow," Trip said breathlessly. "Now *that's* what I call an ice cube."

"Let's hike all the way up to it," suggested Laurel.

Russ frowned. "Going up to it is fine. But I think we'd better turn around once we get up there. It is solid ice, after all."

"So what if it's a little slippery?" Mariah said with a shrug. "I've got good hiking shoes."

"Mariah," Russ insisted, "I really don't think—"

But she'd already gone ahead. "Come on, Trip," she called over her shoulder. "Or are you also afraid of a little ice?"

"Who, me? Afraid?" Already he was leaping from boulder to boulder toward the glacier. "Last one up is a scaredy-cat."

Glancing over at Russ, Laurel saw him shake his head disapprovingly. "You'd think they would've learned by now."

"Well, you certainly don't have to worry about *me* doing anything that stupid." Cassie plopped down on a rock and took a small plastic bag out of her jeans pocket. "Trail mix, anybody?"

Laurel sank down next to her. "Great. So now we sit and wait for the two of them while they show off."

"We might as well take advantage of the opportunity to take a little rest. We've still got the walk back to the car." Russ stretched out on a small patch of grass, folding his arms under his head. "Any more letters from home, Laurel?" he asked conversationally.

"No. Things have been pretty quiet. But thanks for asking."

"Asking what?" Cassie demanded. "I don't get it."

"Oh, Russ happened to walk in on me once when I'd

just gotten a letter from my mother, discussing her general disapproval of my entire life."

Surprised, Cassie glanced at Laurel, then Russ. "Gee, Laurel, are you and *every* male up here—?"

Before Laurel was able to hear her question, a sharp cry cut through the valley. Automatically she raised her eyes upward, toward the glacier.

Instantly she saw what was wrong. Mariah had slipped. She was lying on the smooth surface of the glacier, her face twisted in agony. With one hand she clutched her ankle.

"Help me!" she groaned.

Laurel stood up, shielding her eyes as she watched in horror. Her heart was pounding with fear. Trip was already rushing toward her, barely managing to keep his balance as he clumsily made his way across the ice.

"Should we go up there?" Laurel asked.

"She's probably fine." There was little sympathy in Russ's tone. "Besides, Trip's close enough to help. If she really needs it, that is."

Laurel, Russ, and Cassie stood balanced on giant boulders, watching as Trip helped Mariah across the ice. Fortunately, they hadn't gone that far onto the glacier. Yet traveling even a short distance was proving to be a difficult task.

"What happened?" Laurel demanded as Trip and Mariah got close enough to hear.

"What do you think happened?" Mariah shot back crossly. "I slipped."

"Are you all right?" asked Russ.

"Do I look like I'm all right?" she returned. "My ankle is killing me. I think I broke it. I heard it pop!" When none of the others said anything, she snapped, "Doesn't anybody around here *care*?"

Trip, struggling to bear most of her weight as he

helped her off the glacier, cast her a scathing look. "I vote that we leave her here," said Trip. "I've always though Mariah would make great bear food."

"Very funny." Gingerly she lowered herself onto a boulder.

Russ had taken out his Swiss Army Knife and was using the ice pick on it to cut a chunk out of the glacier. Then he wrapped it in a bandanna he plucked from his pocket. "Here," he said, handing it to Mariah. "Put this on it."

She did as she was told, not bothering to say thank you. "Does anybody have any brilliant ideas about how we're going to get me out of here?"

"I'm afraid you'll have to get out the same way you got in," Russ said simply.

"You're kidding." There was an undertone of disbelief in Mariah's voice. "Can't we just wait for a—a helicopter or a plane to come by—?"

"That simply doesn't happen up here, Mariah."

Looking up at him, she narrowed her eyes accusingly. "You mean to tell me there's no patrol around here, keeping an eye on campers and hikers?"

"I'm afraid not. You seem to be forgetting you're out in the wilds. 'The Last Frontier,' remember?"

"Maybe there are some other hikers who can help."

"We haven't seen anybody since we left the path," Cassie pointed out.

Russ shrugged. "Like I said, there's no choice but for you to walk."

"I-I don't think I can."

"You've got to try," he insisted.

"Here, let me help—" Laurel offered.

"We'll get her," said Russ. He handed her Mariah's backpack. "You can help by carrying this."

Laurel clutched the nylon bag against her chest, biting her lip as she watched Trip and Russ get on either side of Mariah. Slowly, they eased her up to a standing position.

"Try putting your weight on that foot," Russ instructed. "Not too much, now—"

"Ow!" she yelled. "Oh, it hurts!"

Russ glanced at Laurel. "Probably broken."

"Great, just great," said Trip, shaking his head. "How are we ever going to get out of here? We're at least a mile from the Jeep. Probably more."

"I have an idea," said Cassie. "Trip, you're probably the strongest person here. The biggest, anyway. Can you carry Mariah, piggyback?"

"I think I'd rather be left here," Mariah muttered.

"You don't have a lot of choice," Russ pointed out. "Cassie, I think that's an excellent idea."

"Hey, isn't anybody going to ask me what I think?" asked Trip.

"Russ is right," said Laurel. "There's no other way. Unless you can come up with something."

Trip thought for a few seconds, then kicked his backpack in her direction. "Here, carry that. I just hope my back doesn't break."

"Fortunately, we Beverly Hills girls keep ourselves nice and thin," Mariah said with mock sweetness.

"Let's hear it for compulsive dieting." Trip stood in front of her, bending his knees and leaning over. "Hop up, my dear. And congratulations to all of you for being firsthand witnesses of the low point of my entire life."

"Like I'm enjoying this," Mariah muttered as Russ helped her onto Trip's back.

"Hey, you two," Laurel interrupted, "I think we're all stressed out enough without both of you going out of your way to make a bad situation even worse. Do you think you could cool it, at least until we get back to the civilized world?"

She bent down to pick up Trip's backpack. But Russ beat her to it.

"I've got that, Laurel," he said. "You have enough to carry with Mariah's."

"Thanks, Russ." It was comforting to be reminded that at least one civil person was part of this group.

Russ led the way, painstakingly picking out the safest, shortest route. Trip and Mariah were next, with him grunting and panting from the weight on his back and her letting out a yelp of pain every once in a while. Laurel followed, sagging under the weight of two backpacks. Cassie trailed behind, once again putting every ounce of energy she possessed into keeping up with the rest of the group.

They stopped frequently, with Russ helping Mariah slide off Trip's back with only a minimum of jostling. While they clearly needed the breaks, the trip back to the car seemed endless.

Once they were in the Jeep, with Mariah settled into the seat next to the driver, Russ said, "Okay. Now we've made it this far. Our next step is to get Mariah to a doctor."

"How are we ever going to find a doctor?" Cassie demanded. "Have you forgotten that we're in the middle of noplace?"

"I wish Dr. Wells were here," Laurel said, more to herself than to anyone else. "He's been coming to Alaska for years. He'd know where to take her. I wonder if there's some way we could reach him by phone—"

"Just take me back to the cabin," Mariah insisted.

"It's probably just a sprain. I'm sure it'll be fine by to-morrow."

She leaned forward, resting a little bit of her weight on her foot. As she did, she let out a loud yelp of pain.

chapter
fifteen

"That ankle looks pretty bad."

Dr. Wells crouched down at the end of the couch, frowning. Mariah was lying stretched out across it with half a dozen pillows propping up her foot. Gingerly he touched the bruised spot on her skin, meanwhile glancing over to see her reaction. A look of agony crossed her face.

"Maybe if I keep ice on it overnight . . . ?" she suggested feebly.

"This looks like something that's going to require more than ice," Dr. Wells replied. He glanced at his watch. "It's still fairly early. Trip, Laurel, I'd like the two of you to take Mariah into Homer. It's a bit of a drive, but there's an excellent doctor there. I've dealt with Dr. Chase before—and I trust her completely. I'm confident Mariah will get the treatment she needs."

"All right," Laurel agreed.

"I'll give you the address." Dr. Wells stood up, glancing around the cabin. "Anybody have a pencil and paper?"

"In my backpack," Mariah volunteered. "It's right over there, on the table."

Laurel retrieved the backpack and was about to hand it to her when Mariah said crossly, "Just look in the zippered compartment in front."

Sure enough, as Laurel unzipped the front pocket of the nylon bag, she saw a small notebook poking out. She reached inside and felt a pen at the bottom of the compartment.

As she brought it out of the backpack, she froze. It was a size double-zero Rapidograph, a specialized drawing pen that made extremely fine lines. She just stared at it, feeling the blood throbbing at her temples.

The marks made by this kind of pen were just like those on the unsigned note warning her to keep her nose out of the bear-poaching mystery.

I must tell Russ! was the first thought that rushed into her mind. Mariah must be jealous. Maybe she assumes I'm simply trying to make myself look good, showing off in front of Dr. Wells. That would explain her anonymous letter.

But a second, more cautious voice also insisted upon being heard.

This is just circumstantial evidence, the second voice said. You still have no proof that Mariah sent that note. Just a suspicion. . . .

"Can't you find it?" Mariah barked. "Here, give me that—"

"No, I've got them." Laurel handed the pen and pad to Dr. Wells, relieved that no one seemed to have noticed her odd reaction to what she'd discovered in Mariah's backpack.

"Here's the address." Dr. Wells was already jotting it down. He handed it to Laurel. "Now are you sure you two can handle this?"

"Of course," Laurel replied. "Why not?"

Dr. Wells looked at Trip sternly. "I don't want any funny business from you. We've got a serious problem on our hands, and I need you to act responsibly. That means treating both girls with respect."

"Sure, Dr. Wells," Trip assured him. "It'll be fine." Glancing over at Laurel, he added, "Laurel and I have come to an understanding. In fact, we're becoming great friends."

All of a sudden Cassie stood up. Without a word, she stalked into the bedroom.

"Cassie?" Laurel called softly, knocking on the open door as she rounded the corner into the girls' bedroom. "Are you all right?"

The red-haired girl, sprawled facedown across the bottom bunk, didn't even glance up. Her voice muffled by her pillow, she replied, "You're a fine one to ask."

"I don't get it." Gingerly Laurel lowered herself onto the edge of Mariah's cot. "There's clearly something wrong, but you don't seem to want to talk about it—"

"Oh, I'll talk about it." Cassie sat up abruptly. Her face was streaked with tears. "You're an expert, Laurel." She spat out her words. "You could give lessons. In fact, you could write an entire book on the subject."

"I still don't understand."

"I suppose you don't even have to think about it. It just comes to you naturally." In response to Laurel's continued confusion, she added, "You certainly did a nice job of pulling that one off. Arranging things so that Dr. Wells would send you and Trip off to Homer together."

Slowly the meaning of Cassie's words became clear. "Trip and me? I had nothing to do with that! It's not my fault that Mariah—"

"Come on, Laurel. Surely you're not going to deny that you've been after Trip ever since we got up here."

"I do deny it!"

"I've seen the way you come on to him. It's as if you've zeroed in on him, making him your project for the summer. And you're supposed to be my best friend!"

"Cassie, I—"

"You know how I feel about him. But does that stand in your way? Oh, no. Not for a minute. Instead you go right ahead and . . . and *throw* yourself at him—"

"I have absolutely no interest in Trip!" Laurel insisted. "If anything, I'm relieved that he and I seem to have finally reached an understanding. He keeps out of my way and I keep out of his. And when we do end up working together, he more or less behaves himself."

Cassie acted as if she hadn't heard a word Laurel had said. "And now I see you flirting with Russ every chance you get! What is it with you, Laurel? Isn't one boy enough for you? Or do you have some kind of compulsion to make every guy you come into contact with fall in love with you?"

"Neither of them is in love with me!"

"Oh, no? You mean you haven't noticed the way Russ follows you around like a lovesick puppy dog?"

"No, Cassie. I think you're imagining—"

"As for Trip, you're certainly doing your best! At *my* expense, no less! Boy, Laurel. Some friend you turned out to be!"

With that, Cassie jumped off the bed and stomped out of the room. Laurel stayed behind in the bedroom. Her ears were ringing. Was it possible there was any truth in the accusations her best friend had just made? She'd had her own suspicions about Russ, of course . . . but she certainly hadn't chased after him, the way Cassie was implying. As for Trip, she had absolutely no interest in him. She'd been sincere when she'd said she was happy simply to keep things between them as civil as possible.

She stood up, staring out the small window at the

rich greens of the woods surrounding the cabin. Some patches glowed in the sunlight, others were bathed in deep shadows. Usually she found the sight of the forest so comforting. Today, it did nothing to make her feel even the least bit better.

She was dismayed over the possibility that she'd been giving Trip the wrong idea. And that she might be doing something that could hurt Russ. But what mattered to Laurel most was her friendship with Cassie. Now that she finally understood what was getting in their way, she only hoped it wasn't too late to make up for the bad feelings that had sprung up between them.

"Ow! Be careful, will you?" Mariah cast Trip an ice-cold look as he helped her out of the Jeep. "Are you *trying* to torture me, or is it something that just comes to you naturally?"

"Will you keep that stupid ice pack on your foot?" barked Trip. "Or are you *trying* to be difficult?"

Laurel let out a sigh. The ride from the preserve down to Homer should have been a joy. The scenery, after all, had been spectacular as the three of them drove south along the coast of the Kenai Peninsula. The range of mountains across Cook Inlet in the west was still covered with snow all the way down to sea level. And poking up above the range from south to north were three monumental volcanoes, Augustine, Iliamna, and Redoubt. In fact, Mount Redoubt was still steaming from its last eruption.

They even veered off the main road a few times to check out the small seaside village of Ninilchik that Dr. Wells had described. It was little more than a scattering of small buildings, rough wooded houses and a Russian-style church. The only sign of life was the salmon fishermen who lined the water's edge, catching huge fish with apparent ease.

As they stood watching, they suddenly caught sight of a bald eagle, swooping gracefully across the sky. Laurel was amazed at how powerful—and at the same time, how elegant—the bird was.

"Now I appreciate why the eagle was chosen as America's symbol," Laurel observed.

"Once upon a time," said Trip, "bald eagles were found in every state in the union. Now, they're endangered everywhere in the U.S. except Alaska."

When Kachemak Bay came into view, they'd pulled into a special parking area for sightseers. Trip and Laurel jumped out of the car and took turns taking each other's picture beneath a wooden sign made of logs fastened together with rope, reading "Homer, Alaska: Halibut Fishing Capital of the World." In the background was a gently sloping field of colorful wildflowers, leading down to a calm blue expanse of water. Running along the horizon across Kachemak Bay were craggy mountains, a mosaic of blue-gray rock, shimmering snow, and gigantic glaciers that stretched across huge valleys.

Yet aside from a few brief moments when she and Trip had actually been able to relax and drink in their surroundings, Mariah had kept them on edge. She'd complained about everything. The car ride was too long, there were too many twists and turns in the road, the ice pack was too wet, the Jeep was too bumpy. And when she noticed her foot had turned blue, she let out a wail that was like something off the soundtrack of a horror movie.

Now, in response to her complaint that he was handling her too roughly, Trip let out a deep, throaty laugh. "Torturing you is the most natural thing in the world,

Mariah. Now, can you manage to hobble to the front door of the clinic? Or do I have to sling you over my shoulder and carry you?"

"Thanks, I'll just crawl."

"I'll help you, Mariah." Laurel rushed to her side, holding out her arm for Mariah to hang on to. "It's not far."

Mariah barely seemed to be listening. She was eyeing the clinic, a low, wooden building that even Laurel had to admit wasn't exactly the kind of ultramodern medical center she'd been expecting. As a matter of fact, if it hadn't been for the fading sign, "Lindsey Chase, M.D.," next to the door, she never would have guessed this was the clinic Dr. Wells had spoken of so highly.

Yet if there was one thing she'd already learned, it was that nothing in Alaska was the way it was in the rest of the country.

"We're almost there," Laurel said encouragingly. "Just a few more steps—"

"I can see that," Mariah snapped.

The inside of the office was as plain as the outside. The small waiting room was painted light green, furnished with a few wooden chairs. A receptionist sat behind a glass window, typing on a computer. The only noteworthy feature, in fact, was the collection of framed photographs hanging on the wall. One of them, Laurel noticed, was of Dr. Wells.

"Look at this!" she cried. "I didn't realize Dr. Wells and Dr. Chase were such good friends."

They waited only a few minutes before Dr. Chase came out. She was wearing a crisp white lab coat over a pair of jeans and a plaid flannel shirt. She was younger than Laurel had expected, with long straight brown hair, pretty features, and a warm smile.

"Sorry to keep you waiting," she greeted them.

"Ethan called a while ago and said I should keep an eye out for you." Turning to Mariah, she said, "You must be the patient. Come on in to Room Two. It's the first door on your right."

While Mariah was inside with the doctor, Laurel stood in front of the photographs, examining them.

"I bet they're more than friends," she mused.

"Hmmm?" Trip barely glanced up from the fishing magazine he'd picked up from the table and was perusing.

"Dr. Wells and Dr. Chase. I bet they're secretly in love."

Trip cast her a funny look. "Did anyone ever tell you you're a hopeless romantic?"

Laurel could feel her cheeks turning red.

"No, I like it," he insisted. "It's charming. It's nice to know there's somebody in there."

"Somebody in there?" she repeated, not understanding.

"Somebody other than the dedicated scientist," said Trip. "Someone with heart. Someone with soul. Someone who still believes—"

"Excuse me," the receptionist interrupted. She'd just come over to them, a clipboard in hand. "Have you filled out these forms for the patient?"

It wasn't long before Dr. Chase asked Laurel and Trip to come into her office.

"From the looks of things, Mariah's turned her ankle and strained the ligaments pretty badly," she said, folding her hands on the desk in front of her. "If that's the case, she should be back to normal in anywhere from four days to a week.

"However, just to be sure I took an X ray. A fine line showed up on one of the bones. There's a slight possibility she's suffered a hairline fracture. I'm nearly certain it's nothing, but I'd like to have a colleague of mine, Dr. Ellis, take a look at it. I won't be able to get hold of him until tomorrow. Is it possible for the three of you to stay in Homer overnight?"

"Overnight?" Laurel repeated.

"Of course, I'm assuming Dr. Wells will be willing to let you stay out," Dr. Chase added, smiling. "I know how hard Ethan works his students, mainly because he's so passionate about his work." She became lost in thought for a few seconds, her eyes glowing and her cheeks turning pink.

Laurel cast Trip a look that said, "I told you so." Turning back to the doctor, she said, "We'll need a place to stay."

"That's no problem. There's an inn just around the corner. The owner and I are good friends. I'll give him a call and tell him you need a couple of rooms for tonight."

Laurel nodded. "Thank you, Dr. Chase."

"I've set Mariah up with a pair of crutches. It's important that she stay off that foot. I've told her to keep it wrapped in the Ace bandage I've put on, and to keep it elevated. And keep her supplied with as much ice as possible."

Mariah appeared in the doorway, hobbling along on a pair of crutches. "You don't seriously expect me to use these!"

"Sounds like good old Mariah's just fine," breathed Trip.

Waking up early the next morning, Laurel lay in bed for a long time, enjoying her pleasant surroundings. The room she was sharing with Mariah at Homer Lodge was like something from another era. Pale yellow wallpaper sprigged with flowers complemented sheer white cur-

tains that billowed in the breeze wafting through the
open window. The room was sparsely furnished with
twin beds, a dresser, and a sink. A rag rug, pastel
shades of pink and yellow, was centered on the wooden
floor.

It was very restful, and part of her longed to stay
there forever. But she was exhilarated by being in a new
place. She'd loved being at the cabin, far away from all
the trappings and pressures of civilization. Yet now that
she was here in Homer, she was looking forward to
doing a bit of sightseeing.

Less than an hour later, she was doing just that.
Mariah had begrudgingly stayed in bed, her foot elevated. Fortunately, the bookshelf in the lobby contained
a few dozen paperback novels. Laurel picked out three
she thought might interest Mariah and brought them up
to the room with Mariah's breakfast.

"I hate to say this," Laurel said to Trip as they drove
away from the lodge in the Jeep, "but it's kind of a relief, leaving Mariah behind. I know we don't have
much time before Dr. Chase has that report on her X
rays, but I'm anxious to see as much as we can."

"You don't have to sell me," Trip replied. "Well," he
said, "we might as well make the best of this. Let's
check this place out. See some of the sights of the
greater metropolitan area, drive out to the spit and see
what the fishermen are up to—"

"Look! There's a craft gallery," Laurel said, pointing.
"Would you mind pulling in there? I'd love to pick up
something for Cassie."

"First stop, Ptarmigan Craft Gallery." Trip had already stepped on the brake.

The handmade treasures Laurel found in the small
boutique were a surprising contrast to all the natural

wonders she'd been soaking up since her arrival in Alaska. Here was the artwork of a few dozen of Alaska's finest craftspeople. Some of the pieces could have been made anywhere: ceramic bowls glazed in pretty pastels, hand-painted silk scarves, boxes made of stained glass.

Others were pure Alaska. She examined a display of leather bags trimmed with buttons made from caribou antlers, then perused original watercolors of Alaskan wildflowers. Pieces of soapstone had been carved into polar bears and seals. On a variety of items, from pocketbooks to note cards to hollowed-out gourds, were Native American designs, the distinctive renderings of such tribes as the Haida, the Tlingit, and the Kwakiutl. There were so many lovely pieces, so much to admire. Yet nothing seemed quite right for Cassie.

And then a glass case containing silver jewelry caught her eye. Laurel bent over it, studying the earrings, bracelets, and necklaces whose designs incorporated stylized versions of native animals: eagles, ravens, frogs, bears.

"Find something?" Trip asked, coming over and standing at her side.

"I think so." She pointed at a pair of earrings in the corner. "Look at those earrings shaped like eagles. I was so impressed by the eagle we saw coming down, and I love the design. . . . Somehow, I think Cassie would really like those. The shiny silver would look good with her red hair, and since she's such a good artist, I think she'd appreciate the fine craftsmanship. I wonder how much they cost?"

Ten minutes later, Laurel walked out of the store with a small package tucked into her pocket. She was certain that Cassie would be thrilled with her selection. More than that, she hoped the earrings would serve as a sort of peace offering, smoothing over some of the tension that had sprung up between them.

"Where should we go next?" Laurel, sitting in the front seat of the Jeep, peered at the tourist map she'd picked up at the gallery. "It looks as if Homer Spit is one of the high points."

"My thoughts exactly," said Trip.

Laurel glanced over at him. "You're turning out to be an excellent traveling companion."

Trip shrugged. "At your service, ma'am."

Homer Spit was a long, narrow stretch of land that curled into Kachemak Bay. Along the beaches ran an unbroken line of tents, put up by the men and women who stood along the coastline, fishing rods in hand. Further down was a string of buildings connected by a boardwalk that looked as if it had been modeled after a New England fishing village. The dozen or so shops sold everything a visitor might need, from film and T-shirts to bait and fishing tackle. Sprinkled among the stores were rental offices for small fishing boats, as well as scenic cruises across the bay to Gull Island, home to thousands of birds, and Halibut Cove, an isolated artists' colony.

At the end of the spit was a beach. Beyond the calm expanse of Kachemak Bay were the Kenai Mountains, a jagged line of icy white peaks that cut into the horizon. The scene was one of the most magnificent views Laurel had seen since she'd arrived in Alaska. Yet what struck her even more was the black sand.

"Hey, look at this!" Trip held up a piece of seaweed so long it was taller than he was. "Let's bring this with us as a souvenir."

Laurel smiled. This was turning out to be more fun than she'd anticipated. But as she stood on the black beach, enjoying her spectacular surroundings, she suddenly felt guilty. After all, the only reason she and Trip were even here was because of someone else's mishap.

Sighing, she said, "I wonder how Mariah's doing."

"She's probably having a grand old time. After all, she's got her favorite person in the world for company: herself."

"I wonder if Dr. Chase has managed to get in touch with Dr. Ellis yet." Strolling along the water's edge, she said, "You know, I wouldn't be surprised if it turned out I was right."

"About what?"

"About the fact that she and Dr. Wells have a special connection to each other."

"Who knows?" Trip said with a shrug.

"I bet I know what happened," she went on, ignoring his indifference. "A few years ago, they met and fell madly in love. They spent an idyllic summer together. But their great love was destined to fail. He had his career in Vermont, she had hers up here. . . . They were both as passionate about their work as they were about each other. In the end, they agreed never to see each other again because the pain of not being able to be together was simply too great."

For a few moments, Laurel was lost in her little daydream. When she finally glanced up, she saw that Trip was grinning at her.

"You sure have a good imagination."

"Maybe it's this place." She could feel her cheeks turning pink. "You have to admit, there's something very special about Alaska. Something unique."

"You mean like it's the only place where you can find eagles, the only place where the seaweed is more than six feet long—"

"It's much more than that. Here, you're free to be yourself, whatever that happens to be. There's no one looking over your shoulder, constantly reminding you how you're supposed to act. Nobody's scolding you, saying you 'should' do this and you 'should' do that. You're completely on your own. There are no rules, no limits. . . ."

She expected Trip to laugh at her. Yet when she dared to cast him a shy glance, she found that the expression on his face was serious. "You really think about things, don't you?"

"I don't know. I suppose I do."

"I like that. I haven't met many girls who are that introspective."

Laurel could feel anger rising up inside her. But before she had a chance to protest, Trip held up his hands.

"Wait a minute. Don't get all huffy. I was merely making an observation, that's all. You're not like most girls."

"Trip, you talk about girls as if they were creatures from another planet."

"Sometimes I think they are. I don't know; maybe it's partly my fault. I suppose it could be the way I come across that makes most girls act the way they do around me."

Laurel remained guarded. "And exactly how do they act?"

"They flirt with me. Tease me." He shrugged. "It's like . . . it's like it's all part of some game we're playing. Nobody takes it very seriously. We're all just playing different roles, that's all. I say something suggestive, the girl I'm talking to says something back. . . . It's fun, but I guess it's not really a good way for me to get to know her." He gazed out across the bay. "I don't know; maybe I've been missing out on something all these years."

"My goodness, Trip. You're certainly full of surprises." Laurel's reaction was sincere. "It's hard for me to admit this, but I think I might have misjudged you."

"What do you mean?"

"Maybe there really is a thinking, feeling person in there, underneath that Don Juan facade of yours."

"Aw, come on, Laurel," said Trip. "I'm not that different from anyone else. Oh, sure, I come on a little strong sometimes. But that's because I don't know any other way to act around girls."

"Let me ask you something," Laurel said thoughtfully. "Have you ever had a girl who was a friend?"

He looked puzzled. "I've had a girlfriend ever since I was in the fifth grade."

"I'm not talking about a girlfriend. I'm talking about a girl who's a friend. One that you're not dating, just one who you treat like any other friend."

Trip thought for a few seconds. "You know, I don't think I have."

"Well, maybe you and I could try being friends."

"I don't think I could do that, Laurel."

"Why not?"

"Because I'm just too crazy about you." He'd stopped walking, and as he turned to face her, he placed his hands on her shoulders.

"Trip, I—"

"I mean it, Laurel," he said, his soft voice more tender than she'd ever heard it. "I really am crazy about you. You're really special. You're not like any other girl I've ever met."

Laurel's heart was pounding. She knew he was going to kiss her. And while part of her warned her to push him away, another part wanted him to. Perhaps she really had misjudged him. Maybe he did come on so strong because he didn't know any other way to approach girls. She owed him the benefit of the doubt. . . .

Leaning forward, she turned her face upward to meet his. The initial touch of his lips was electrifying. Yet as she kissed him back, she realized that the pounding of her heart was due only to her surprise, and nothing more.

"Trip," she muttered, taking a step back, "I'm not sure this is what I want. I-I feel so confused—"

"Take your time, Laurel. I don't want to pressure you. It's just that . . ." His hands still on her shoulders, he looked around at the bay and, across the way, the magnificent mountains. "It's just like you said. Alaska *is* special. Being here is making me see things with a whole new perspective."

She looked up into his eyes, struggling to sort out what she was feeling. All along she'd found him boorish and insensitive, but all of a sudden she was seeing a new side of him, one she'd never even dreamed existed.

"I need more time," she told him. "All this is happening too fast."

"Okay." He ran one finger lightly alongside her cheek. "We'd better get back to the lodge."

"I-I feel like I don't want to leave."

Trip's eyes were shining as he gazed down at her. "Don't worry. We have all the time we need."

Laurel still felt as if she were in a dream, wrapped in a mixture of astonishment and confusion, as she went upstairs to check on Mariah. Dr. Chase had telephoned to say Dr. Ellis's evaluation of the X rays was the same as hers: the ankle had been sprained, with no break in the bone. Mariah had used her crutches to hobble around the room, packing. She was itching to get out, marveling over the fact that she was actually looking forward to getting back to the preserve.

"I'll go tell Trip we can check out of our rooms," Laurel volunteered. "He's waiting in the lobby."

Coming down the stairs, she could hear his voice. As she turned the corner and his words became clear, she froze.

"I bet a girl like you who's lived here all your life could show me some great places," he was saying. "So what do you think? If I can come up with an excuse to get back here in the next couple of days . . ."

Trip was leaning against the front desk, talking softly to the young woman working there. Laurel stood in silence, staring.

"I'll tell you what," she heard him say. "How about if I give you a call here at the lodge in the next day or two and—"

He happened to glance up then, spotting Laurel. He cut off his words midsentence. She expected him to react: to turn red, to start sputtering, to apologize. Instead, he smiled.

"Hi, Laurel. I was just getting to know some of the local folks."

"So I see," she returned coldly. "I'm afraid you're out of time. Mariah's ready to leave. You'll no doubt be pleased to hear she didn't break any bones."

"Great." Trip grinned at her. "Then we can be on our way. I'll be right up to help Mariah get down the stairs."

Laurel turned her back on him, her cheeks burning. Before she did, she caught sight of him winking at the girl behind the desk.

chapter
sixteen

I won't think about it. I just won't let myself think about it.

Cassie pushed a strand of curly red hair behind one ear and studied the sketch pad that lay balanced on her bended knees. She leaned her head against the big cottonwood tree a few hundred feet beyond the cabin, ignoring the roughness of the bark just as stubbornly as she ignored the stinging in her eyes while she struggled to keep tears from falling.

She knew perfectly well that as she sat in the woods, trying to force herself to stop thinking about anything besides the clump of fireweed she was attempting to draw, Laurel was in Homer with Trip. And the burning in the pit of her stomach was only partly because of her feelings for Trip. Even more, she was reeling from having been betrayed by Laurel.

My best friend! she thought. At least she was *supposed* to be my best friend. . . .

The same strand of hair fell forward into her face again. With the same determination, Cassie swept it away. She'd decided she'd spent enough time thinking about those two. For now, she wanted to escape into the white page in front of her.

A line here, some shading there. . . . Before long, the rest of the world ceased to exist. There was only her rendering of the dramatic pink wildflower, each detail captured with a fine drawing pencil, the colors replicated with pastels. For the moment, the only thing that mattered was getting it just right.

Suddenly a shadow fell across the sheet of white paper in front of her. Abruptly Cassie snapped her head up.

"Oh, it's you," she said to Russ, partly relieved, partly annoyed.

"Sorry. I didn't mean to scare you."

She shrugged noncommittally, then bent over her sketch once again. But the fun had already gone out of it. The presence of someone else made it impossible for her to concentrate.

"What are you doing out here?" she asked, her impatience only thinly masked.

Russ held up the binoculars he'd been carrying at his side. "Dr. Wells sent me out to watch the terns."

"Uh, oh," Cassie commented, remembering Mariah's harrowing experience. "I hope you're prepared for an attack."

"Fortunately, I know what they'll put up with—and what they won't. Actually, terns are very interesting birds." He was growing more and more animated. "Did you know they spend the winter months in Argentina, then fly all the way up here to Alaska to mate in the spring? It's the longest annual migration of any bird in the world."

Cassie peered at Russ more closely, shielding her eyes against the sun. "You really know a lot about nature, don't you?"

Russ averted his eyes. "Yeah, I guess. I mean, I did grow up on a preserve, and when you spend so much time around something—"

"But it's more than that. You really *love* it."

His face and neck had turned pink.

"I think it's great," Cassie said quickly. "It's important to have something in your life that you're passionate about. Most people aren't lucky enough to have that one thing they get really excited about." Suddenly shy, she added, "I feel that way about art."

"Really?" Russ looked at her intently. He'd put the binoculars down gently on a soft pile of leaves and lowered himself onto a large flat rock. "Is that why you're always sneaking around with that pad of yours?"

"I don't sneak!" Cassie was indignant. "I-I just don't expect anybody else to understand, that's all. Besides, I'm not exactly crazy about other people looking over my shoulder all the time, wanting to see what I'm doing and asking me a million questions—"

"I guess that means you're not going to show me what you're working on."

Cassie hesitated. "Well, I—"

"You don't have to. I mean, I understand if you feel funny showing your artwork to me. But I really am interested. Dr. Wells has been raving about what a terrific artist you are."

"He has?" Cassie's surprise was genuine.

"Sure. I heard him telling Trip and Mariah what a bonus it is for his research that he has you to draw such great pictures of the flora and fauna around the lake. He said he's hoping to include some of them in the articles he writes about his research."

"I-I had no idea." Cassie could feel her own cheeks turning red.

"Maybe now that you know what a good artist you are, you won't be so shy about showing me your work." Russ's tone had become teasing.

Yet instead of squirming under his attention, Cassie

could feel her bashfulness fading. "If you're really that interested."

"I am," he said simply.

She paused only a moment before handing over her sketch pad. Anxiously she watched his face as he studied the drawing she'd been working on, then flipped over the pad to the beginning and looked through the two dozen or so she'd made in the past few days. His expression was earnest. His mouth was drawn into a straight line and his eyes were intense as they lingered over each rendering she'd made: birds, flowers, grasses, small animals, even fish.

"Well?" she finally asked, unable to wait any longer. "What do you think?"

"Wow," he said breathlessly.

Cassie laughed nervously. " 'Wow,' as in 'Wow, these are good,' or 'Wow' as in 'Wow, these are awful'?"

His expression still dead serious, Russ handed the sketch pad back to Cassie. " 'Wow,' as in, 'These drawings are as good as any I've ever seen.' And that includes professional journals, textbooks—"

Cassie blinked. "You're not joking, are you?"

"You're good, Cassie. You're really good."

She broke into a wide grin. "So Dr. Wells knew what he was talking about, after all."

"Have you thought about becoming a professional artist?"

"I-I never thought I was good enough. Drawing's always just been a hobby."

"I may not know much about art—in fact, I don't know a *thing* about art—but I do know something about technical drawing. And like I've already said, your stuff is excellent. If I were you, I'd give serious thought to getting into technical drawing. You could make a real contribution."

Russ leaned over and picked up his binoculars. "Speaking of making a contribution, I'd better get back to my tern watching. The data base has to include two hours of observation every day."

Cassie felt a pang of disappointment as she watched him walk away. She was surprised by what he'd said about her artwork. It made her feel good to be complimented so enthusiastically.

But even more, she was surprised at how much she'd enjoyed talking to him. Shy, quiet Russ ... was it possible there was more to him than just some geeky guy who got excited about nature?

She watched him until he'd disappeared into the woods, then with a little shrug turned back to her drawing.

Laurel, Trip, and Mariah drove back from Homer in silence, tension hanging over them like a rain cloud. As the Jeep rounded the bend and the cabin came into sight, Laurel muttered, "It's good to be back."

She hopped out of the car, leaving Trip to help Mariah. After thirty-six hours, she'd had enough of both of them. With the small package from the Ptarmigan Craft Gallery tucked into the front pocket of her backpack, she headed into the cabin to find Cassie.

She found her in their bedroom, sitting at the edge of the bottom bunk. Thirty or forty of her drawings were spread out across the mattress haphazardly.

"Hi," she said shyly, pausing in the doorway.

Cassie barely glanced up. "Hello, Laurel."

"What are you doing?"

"Organizing my drawings." She hesitated before adding, "Dr. Wells is going to sit down with me and go over them. He wants to make sure I'm covering all the different species of plants and animals he wants."

"Great." Gingerly Laurel sat down on the cot. "Well, it turns out Mariah's ankle is only sprained. There are no bones broken. She's supposed to keep off her foot for a few days."

Cassie remained focused on her sorting. She was making one pile of wildflowers, another of birds, one more of insects, stacking the pictures with the greatest care.

"You know," Laurel went on, "I actually feel sorry for Mariah. I know she's been a pain ever since day one. But the truth is that she's had one bad experience after another. I suppose she brought a lot of it on herself, but even so, I can't blame her for being upset.

"This must have been the last straw for her. Imagine, being all the way up here and spraining your ankle. She must be so disappointed that she won't be able to keep up with the rest of us! Besides, it must be kind of scary, getting hurt so far away from home. . . ."

She let her voice trail off, aware that Cassie wasn't listening. It was as if there were a barrier between them, an invisible wall that couldn't be seen but that could easily be felt. Laurel wanted desperately to break through.

Suddenly she snapped her fingers. "Your present! I almost forgot!"

Cassie glanced up, surprised. "You brought me a present?"

"It's just a little souvenir from Homer."

Reaching into her backpack and rummaging around, she brought out the small white box. On top was a sticker printed with the name of the gallery.

"Open it," she urged, eager to see Cassie's reaction.

Cassie's expression was one of astonishment. Slowly she took the lid off the cardboard box, then lifted out the earrings Laurel had so painstakingly chosen for her. She peered at them, her expression blank.

"I hope you like them," Laurel said, suddenly uneasy about Cassie's lack of enthusiasm for what she'd thought was a perfectly lovely pair of earrings. "I had a feeling that out of all the jewelry I looked at, you'd like these earrings best. They also had some pretty necklaces. I was pretty sure you'd prefer these, but Trip thought you'd like—"

"Trip?" Cassie repeated coldly.

Laurel froze. She realized she'd made a major mistake in mentioning him. "That's right."

"You went shopping with Trip?"

"Yes. Poor Mariah was resting at the hotel, waiting for Dr. Chase to get a second opinion on her X rays—"

"You two practically had a honeymoon in Homer, didn't you?"

Laurel took a deep breath. "Cassie, we really have to talk about this. Please let me explain—"

"It could hardly have been more cozy, could it? You and Trip painting the town red while Mariah was tucked away at some hotel. . . . Meanwhile I was back here, miles away. . . ."

"You've got to understand that I'm simply not interested in Trip."

"But he's crazy about you!" Cassie's voice was edged with hysteria.

"Cassie, the last thing you need in your life is a boy like Trip."

"What's wrong with him?"

"I don't know where to start! He's conceited, he's arrogant, he thinks he's God's gift to women. . . . And while we're on the subject of women, he seems to think they belong somewhere down there with trained dogs and other house pets."

Laurel paused, wondering how much she dare tell Cassie. She could see she wasn't getting anywhere with her. Yet she couldn't be sure how she'd take it if she told her what had really happened in Homer. . . .

Just as she was about to pour out the entire story, Mariah burst into the room, nearly falling over herself as she struggled with her crutches.

"That's it!" she cried. "That's the last straw!"

"What happened?" Laurel asked.

Mariah didn't seem to hear. "I've had enough. I've put up with that creep long enough. I'm fed up with Trip, and—and everything else about this place!"

"What did Trip do now?" Laurel asked angrily.

"He thinks it's hilarious to call me every insulting name in the book. Peg leg, gimp . . . you'd think that boy grew up in a cave. He's the cruelest, most insensitive person I've ever met."

Choking on her words, Mariah threw down her crutches. Angrily she started grabbing her clothes and stuffing them into her duffel bag.

"What are you doing?" Cassie demanded.

"I'm getting out of here. This whole trip has been a disaster from the very start." Mariah spat out her words. "It was a mistake. An awful, horrible, *stupid* mistake!"

Her face was hidden by the curtain of her long black hair as she hopped around the cabin, thrusting things into the duffel bag. Laurel sat in silence, perched on the edge of the cot, watching.

"Ever since I got here, I've had one horrible experience after another. First, the attack of the killer terns. Next, finding dead bears at every turn. Then those disgusting leeches all over my body. And now spraining my ankle. And I haven't even mentioned all the egos I've had to deal with."

"Mariah," Laurel finally said, her voice soft, "don't

forget that there've been good moments as well. What about the beauty of this place? What about the chance to work with a scientist as accomplished as Dr. Wells? What about all you've learned, for heaven's sake?"

"Oh, no, you don't." Mariah waved her hand in the air dismissively. "Don't think for a minute I'm going to fall for that goody–two-shoes act of yours. It's true I came here to learn something about science. At least that was part of how I got roped into this in the first place. But if you ask me if it's been worth it, there's absolutely no question in my mind that this has been the most horrendous experience of my entire life!"

"At the very least, wait until your foot's healed," Laurel pleaded. "Come on, Mariah. Give it more time."

Suddenly Mariah stopped. She turned around to face Laurel, a look of amazement on her face. "Why are you doing this, Laurel? What difference does it make to you whether I stay or go?"

"I-I'm not really sure." Laurel frowned. "I guess it's because I've come to think of you as part of the group. For better or for worse, we're all in this together. It's hard to imagine being up here without you and Russ . . . even Trip." With a little shrug, she added, "We're a team."

Mariah hesitated, standing in the middle of the room with a sweater in her hand. "It really matters to you, doesn't it?"

Laurel thought for a few seconds, then nodded.

"You never cease to amaze me." There was no anger in Mariah's words. Instead, she sounded sincere.

"Please stay, Mariah," said Laurel.

"The doctor *did* tell me to rest my foot for a few days. . . ."

"You don't want to make it worse," Laurel said gently. "A long plane ride would be torture."

With a loud sigh, Mariah plopped down on the bed. "I don't know what to do. I just feel so—so helpless."

"I can imagine. And nobody knows as well as I do what a jerk Trip can be," Laurel went on. "Don't let him get you down." Glancing at Cassie, she added, "If anything, the three of us have got to stick together just so we can demolish his theory that girls aren't as good as boys."

"I suppose that if I left," Mariah mused, "in a way it'd be saying he'd won."

"That's right. You don't want him to think he drove you out."

"All right," Mariah finally said. "I'll stay."

"Good," Laurel said simply. "I think you're making the right choice."

She glanced over at Cassie once again. Her blue eyes were clouded. Yet instead of avoiding Laurel's gaze, she looked right back at her. Laurel couldn't be sure, but she thought that what she saw reflected there was admiration.

chapter
seventeen

When Dr. Wells came into the cabin early the next morning, he was carrying a letter. The look on his face told Laurel he had something favorable to report.

"Good news," he told the group, gathered around the table eating breakfast. "I just got a note from Ben Seeger. We've been invited to Anchorage to give a presentation on our research at the Department of Fish and Game."

"That should give you a good chance to get some feedback on our tern research," said Laurel. "When are you going?"

"I'm not. The invitation's for this Friday, and John Torvold and I've already made plans to go into Seward to get supplies and meet with some other field biologists. But this is an excellent opportunity for a couple of you to get out there and talk about what we've been doing."

"Sounds great." Trip was grinning broadly. "What time do I leave?"

"I'm afraid only Laurel and Russ will be going."

Glancing around the table, Laurel saw that Trip's face had fallen. She wasn't at all surprised to see that Cassie looked relieved. What did surprise her was that Mariah looked almost as disappointed as Trip.

182

"This is a really excellent opportunity," Mariah said. "Wouldn't it make sense for us all to go?"

"I can't spare all of you for a full day. The summer is speeding by, and we still have a lot to accomplish before the end of our stay. I can only afford to send two of you. Besides," he added, casting a stern look at Mariah, "you're still supposed to keep off that foot."

Laurel glanced over at Mariah, intending to cast her a look of sympathy. Yet when she did, the intensity with which Mariah's dark eyes were burning kept her from doing so.

"Well, Laurel," Mariah commented, speaking so softly the others couldn't hear, "it looks like you lucked out. You seem to have a real talent for coming out on top."

Laurel's first reaction was to defend herself. Not only did she feel betrayed, she also felt foolish. To think she'd actually thought she'd gotten through to Mariah the day before. It turned out that nothing had changed.

She simply looked away, shaking her head slowly. It was time, she knew, to start accepting the fact that no matter how hard she tried, she couldn't keep Mariah from being Mariah.

With an exasperated sigh, Cassie threw down her drawing pencil and reached up to stretch her arms. With Laurel and Russ working with Dr. Wells on their presentation and Mariah still bedridden, she'd decided to throw herself into her sketches for the project. For almost an hour she'd been sitting cross-legged at the edge of the lake, bent over her sketch pad. Yet today nothing was coming out right. Her flowers looked two-dimensional, the leaves lifeless . . . even the proportions were all wrong.

She was about to give up for the day, to go back to

the cabin and settle in with a good book and one of the chocolate bars she'd kept stashed away. But as she stood up and brushed leaves from her jeans, she noticed a flash of color moving among the trees a hundred yards or so deeper into the woods.

It only took her a few seconds to figure out it was Trip. Easily she made out his familiar outline in the distance: his broad shoulders, his muscular torso, his headful of blond curls that had been in need of a trim at the beginning of the trip and now was positively unruly.

Cassie's heartbeat quickened. Part of her, her shy, uncertain side, yearned to run and hide, to head back to the cabin before he spotted her. Yet another part of her, a brave part she'd barely realized existed, was thrilled to have finally gotten him alone.

She smoothed her short red curls, wondering how she looked. This was a moment she'd been anticipating for a long time. If only she could let him know how she felt. If instead of being so bashful and tongue-tied in his presence, she could flirt with him, tease him . . . make him see her in an entirely different light. . . .

After running her fingers through her hair one more time, wanting to make sure no leaves or twigs were stuck there, she tucked her sketchbook under her arm and headed in his direction, taking extra care not to embarrass herself by stumbling.

He was crouched in a clearing, frowning as he studied a notebook, comparing what he saw on the page with something he was examining on the ground. His hair was pale blond, Cassie noted, bleached by his having spent so many hours in the summer sun. He wore faded jeans and a torn gray sweatshirt, the fabric stretched taut across his wide shoulders.

"Hello, Trip." Cassie did her best to sound casual.

She only hoped he couldn't hear the jackhammer-like pounding of her heart.

He barely glanced up. "Hey, Cassie. How's it going?"

"Great." She paused, wishing desperately she could come up with something to say that was interesting enough to pull him away from his book.

"How are your observations?" she asked.

"Hmmm?" He barely seemed to have noticed that she'd spoken.

"I said, How's the research going?"

"Oh. Fine. I'm finding. . . . Would you please move? You're blocking the sunlight, and I really want to get a better look at this mushroom. I'm having trouble identifying it."

Cassie's mind was racing. She wanted so desperately to connect with Trip, to make him respond in a way that showed he considered her worthy of at least some of his attention.

"Trip," she said boldly, "would you like to go for a canoe ride on the lake some evening? Just the two of us?"

"If I'd only thought to bring one of my field guidebooks along, I'd be able to key this out. . . ." It wasn't until he'd spent a good minute or two examining the clump of mold that he glanced up. "Did you say something about going for a ride on the lake? What are you talking about?"

"I just thought . . . I only . . . what I meant was. . . ." Cassie could feel her face turning bright red. "So you and I could talk."

"Talk? About what?"

"Well, it's not what we'd talk about so much. It's more that, uh, you and I haven't really had much of a chance to get to know each other."

He stood up, frowning as he stared at her. Cassie

wished the ground would swallow her up, but she forced herself to look into his eyes, waiting for his response.

"Sorry, Cassie. I don't have time for any joyrides today. Could you hand me my backpack? I'd better run back to the cabin for that field guide so I can get going with this. Catch you later!"

He was gone as abruptly as he'd appeared. Swallowing hard in an attempt to get rid of the lump in her throat, Cassie tucked her sketchbook into her backpack. She knew she'd never be able to concentrate. At the moment, she didn't even feel like eating that chocolate bar. Instead, she headed further into the woods, hoping that a long walk by herself might help banish the confusion and other bad feelings that were rumbling around inside her like a summer storm.

Cassie stepped through the dense growth of forest, into the clearing just beyond Wolf Lake. She paused at the edge, struck by how peaceful it was here. The field of muskeg with its coarse, uneven growth was particularly beautiful today. The oblique light of the sun, shining weakly in a blue-gray sky, brought out the subtle variations in the muted shades of green, yellow, and red.

But the beauty that surrounded her was not what she was thinking about as she stood alone in the field. Her heart ached too much for her to concentrate on the magnificent view. She couldn't remember having ever felt such a yearning. And knowing she would never be able to have the one thing she truly wanted caused tears of frustration to well up in her eyes.

She started when she noticed someone off in the distance, coming toward her. She watched as Russ moved with great determination across the spongy ground, raising his hand in a wave as he drew near. He was carrying a pair of binoculars, a field guide tucked under his arm.

"Hey, Cassie," he called, smiling broadly at her. "How's it going?"

"Oh, all right, I guess."

"Great day, isn't it? Perfect for bird-watching. I saw five or six new species. I can hardly wait to tell Dr. Wells. . . ."

Suddenly his voice trailed off. He was close to her now, and he leaned forward, his face tensing into a frown. "Are you okay?"

Cassie's first impulse was to assure him that everything was just fine. Instead, she found herself saying, "Not really."

"What's the matter? Are you feeling all right?"

"It's nothing like that. It's just that. . . ." She buried her face in her hands. "Oh, Russ. What's wrong with me?"

The sympathetic look on his face changed to one of confusion. "What are you talking about, Cassie? There's nothing wrong with you."

"There must be." She bit her lip, not certain of how honest she dared be with Russ. "I must be the only girl in the universe that Trip's not interested in."

"Is *that* it." His expression softened. "Why don't we find someplace to sit down?"

She nodded, then followed him to the edge of the field of muskeg, where the woods began. Once they'd each found a fallen log to sit on, he shrugged off his backpack and lowered it to the ground.

"You know," he said earnestly, "I'd kind of noticed you were interested in Trip."

Cassie laughed coldly. "I didn't know it was that obvious."

He shrugged. "I'm pretty good at picking up on people's signals." He hesitated before adding, "What I haven't been able to figure out is *why*."

"What do you mean, why?"

"Don't get me wrong. I think Trip's a really bright guy. He's serious about science, and he knows what he's doing. He and I pretty much get along fine. It's just that when it comes to the way he acts around girls. . . ." Russ shook his head. "Like I said, Cassie, I can't figure out what you see in him."

"That's my business," she replied tartly.

"I suppose it is. It's just that . . . well, somehow I see a girl like you ending up with a guy who's practically the total opposite of Trip."

"Oh, I get it. You mean somebody short, dark, and ugly."

"No. I mean somebody quiet. Sensitive. Considerate. Somebody who'd appreciate you, Cassie."

She made a face. "What's there to appreciate?"

Russ just stared. "You're kidding, right?"

"As if I have anything to offer."

"Cassie, you've got lots to offer! You're a really special girl!"

She blinked in surprise. *"Me?"*

He smiled gently. "I'm surprised you don't have a better sense of that, Cassie."

"Oh, I get it. You mean because I can draw pretty well."

"No. Your talent in art is only one small part of you. What matters even more is the kind of person you are. I mean, look at you. You're bright and considerate and interested in other people. . . . And you're attractive, too."

Cassie snapped her head up. She saw that Russ had turned beet red. "Why, thanks, Russ."

He shrugged, keeping his eyes down. "I'm surprised

you don't already know all this, Cassie," he said, his voice thick with embarrassment.

Before she had a chance to reply, he'd jumped up off the log and headed toward the field of muskeg.

"Here, let me show you something," he said, beckoning.

Cassie followed him, puzzled. He was pointing at tiny, odd-looking plants about the size of a quarter that dotted the moist green muskeg. Green rounded leaves, tinged with red, were covered with minuscule bristles, glistening in the sunlight.

She blinked. "What are those?"

"Examples of the genus *Drosera*."

"Huh?"

"They're called sundew plants."

"That's a pretty name."

"A pretty name for a plant with a real attitude."

"What do you mean?"

"These guys are carnivorous. Or to be more accurate, insectivorous."

"You mean they eat bugs?"

"Insects," he corrected her gently.

Cassie's eyes widened. "You mean like a Venus's-flytrap?"

"Sort of. I'm afraid these guys aren't as dramatic. They don't close around their victims. They trap them with the sticky fluid on their tentacles, then absorb the nutrients. Here, watch this." Crouching down, he searched the muskeg until he found a mosquito. He placed it on the tentacles.

Cassie watched in fascination as the mosquito struggled to free itself from the sappy threads that bound it to the top of the sundew's leaf. "Wow! That's incredible! A plant that eats animals!"

"Pretty cool, huh? How'd you like a garden full of these?" he joked.

She laughed. "I guess you wouldn't have to worry about bugs eating your flowers." She grew serious as she examined the plant more closely. "They're so pretty, though. No, not really pretty ... it's more like they're interesting looking."

"Yet, there's much more to them than you'd think. At first glance, they look like just any old plant. But once you know something about them, they're fascinating."

Russ plucked one out and handed it to Cassie. "Here you go. Why don't you press one of these in a book? Maybe it'll be a helpful reminder that there's more to most things than meets the eye."

Gratefully Cassie accepted the sundew plant.

Russ stood up and stretched. "Enough on the lessons nature can teach us. I've got a lot more territory to cover before the day is through. If you'll excuse me, I'll be off."

"Okay, Russ. Catch you later."

As Cassie watched him head off in another direction, looking very much at ease with himself as he slogged confidently through the muskeg with his pack on his back and his binoculars around his neck, her mind was clouded.

Why is it so easy to have fun with Russ, she thought, while being around Trip makes me feel clumsy and unattractive ... like the fat little girl I used to be the whole time I was growing up?

She shook her head thoughtfully. While she'd hoped coming out here into the woods would help put an end to some of her confusion, instead she was feeling more bewildered than ever.

chapter
eighteen

"It's amazing," mused Laurel as she stared out the window of the Jeep in fascination. "Compared to Washington, D.C., Anchorage is a very small city. Yet after living at Wolf Lake for so long, being back in civilization is actually intimidating!"

"I know what you mean," Russ agreed, glancing over from the driver's seat. "It's startling to see all these people crammed together in one place. At the lake, seeing even one person you don't readily recognize would be a shock!"

Still, Laurel's initial uneasiness over being in a city faded quickly, giving way to excitement over being in a new place. She and Russ had made a point of leaving the Kenai Peninsula early that morning, wanting to be certain there'd be time for sightseeing before their three o'clock presentation at the Department of Fish and Game.

The city of Anchorage was surprisingly small, roughly ten-square blocks. The buildings were low, with a frontier-town feeling to them. A few log cabins still stood in the downtown area, tucked between buildings of a much more recent vintage. There were a few familiar sights; she actually let out a little cry when they drove past Woolworth's. But most of the businesses they passed had local roots.

When Russ pulled the Jeep into a parking space on 4th Avenue, one of Anchorage's main streets, Laurel jumped out. She looked around, eagerly drinking in everything around her. This street was a center for tourists. In fact, right across the street was an authentic-looking log cabin with a big sign reading "Visitor Information Center" above the door. What was most striking about the small building was the roof. It was a sod roof, covered with thick green grass.

While shops selling postcards, T-shirts, and mugs dominated 4th Avenue, there were some specialty shops that Laurel and Russ found much more intriguing as they wandered along the sidewalk. Among them were galleries selling Alaskan handicrafts. Browsing in one of them, catching sight of a display of silver earrings, Laurel felt a twinge of sadness. The last time she'd been in such a store, when she was in Homer, she'd tried to make amends with Cassie. Yet the tension between them had remained high.

She tried to push all that aside and instead concentrate on enjoying herself. When she noticed some handmade Eskimo dolls, she spent a long time admiring them, finally deciding to indulge in one for herself.

After looking around the shops for a while, Laurel realized she was getting hungry. She was about to suggest to Russ that they start looking for a place to have lunch when a familiar sign caught her eye.

"Look!" she cried. "McDonald's! I guess there really *are* things I miss about the civilized world!"

Eating in the familiar spot was a welcome break from roughing it. Still, Laurel was taken aback by how modern everything seemed. The bright lights, the Formica tables and plastic seat covers on the seats . . . even the drinking straws, each one individually wrapped in paper. What a contrast it was to the simple, almost primitive life she'd gotten used to. She found herself missing the cabin and the lake. There she felt free. Here, she was beginning to feel closed in.

She and Russ sat down opposite each other at a table with a fake wood-grain finish. Thoughtfully munching her french fries, Laurel gazed out the window. She had a perfect view of one of the tourist shops right across the street. Its display window was crowded with T-shirts, mugs, and posters that were already starting to look familiar. Most of them, she noted, featured pictures of wildlife.

How ironic it is, she thought, that these garish items don't even begin to capture the spectacular beauty of Alaska. It's going to be so hard leaving all this behind, once it's time to get back. . . .

"Earth to Laurel."

The sound of Russ's voice snapped her out of her thoughtful state.

"Sorry." She smiled at him apologetically. "I guess I wasn't being very good company."

"You're always good company. I was just wondering what you were thinking about."

"I was thinking about how magnificent Alaska is. And how those T-shirts and mugs do absolutely nothing to capture any of it."

Biting into his Big Mac, he shrugged. "We're lucky. A lot of people who come to Alaska never really get to experience it. They end up viewing it all through the windows of a tour bus."

"It's funny. Today, for the first time since we came, I feel like a tourist, instead of like someone who really belongs here." Taking a sip of her milkshake, Laurel gestured toward the street. "Have you gotten used to being in a city yet?"

Russ laughed. "All my life, I've felt strange in cities. Anchorage is no exception."

"I can't get over the fact that this McDonald's looks like every other McDonald's in the country. Right now we could be anywhere."

"But we're not. We're in Anchorage, Alaska. And we might as well use the couple of hours we've got before our talk to enjoy it."

He stood up and reached for her hand. "Let's paint this town red."

For the next two hours, Laurel and Russ did their best to see all they could. At the Anchorage Museum of History and Art, they viewed life-size depictions of life in various parts of the state at different points in history. There was also an impressive display of paintings of Alaskan scenery, many done by well-known artists.

Next they did some more shopping at the 5th Avenue Mall. Laurel bought a beaded belt for her father and a leather purse for her mother. She suspected that both would go unused, but she didn't want to go home empty-handed.

They would have liked to have seen more, but when Russ checked his watch they discovered the time had passed more quickly than they'd realized.

"We'd better get back to the car and head over to Fish and Game," he said. "I wouldn't mind showing up a little early."

Laurel nodded. "Good idea. I could use the chance to go over our notes one more time before we get up in front of all those people to speak."

Russ was silent as they walked toward the car. Laurel assumed he was thinking about the presentation. Yet when he finally spoke, his voice sounded odd.

"You know," he said slowly, "I really had a good time today."

"I did, too," said Laurel. "It was great seeing Anchorage. Maybe playing tourist every once in a while isn't so bad, after all."

"That's not exactly what I meant." Russ hesitated. "I-I meant I had a good time spending the day . . . with you."

Slowly his meaning became clear. Laurel swallowed hard. "It was fun," she said noncommittally.

"I-I'm really glad I've got to know you," he went on in the same deliberate way. He kept his eyes down as they walked. "As far as I'm concerned, that turned out to be one of the best things about this whole trip."

"I'm glad you and I became friends this summer, too," she replied, choosing her words with great care. "I've learned a lot from you. And, well, having you as part of the research team has been really fun."

"But there's something I've been wanting to tell you, Laurel." He hesitated, taking a deep breath. "I—"

Gently Laurel placed her hand on his arm. "Russ?"

"Yes?"

"Don't. We have to give our presentation in just a few minutes. Let's concentrate on that."

"But what about . . . what about you and me?"

"I'm glad we're friends, Russ. And I'm looking forward to you and me staying friends, even after we've gotten back to school."

There was a long pause before he said, "Sure." The thickness in his voice told her she'd gotten her point across.

"You're a special guy, Russ," she went on. "And one of these days, some really special girl's going to recognize that." Chuckling, she added, "If she's smart, she'll grab hold of you so fast you won't know what hit you. And I predict the two of you will live happily ever after."

Russ laughed self-consciously. "That's funny. A few days ago I said practically the same words to Cassie."

"Did you mean it?"

He thought for a few seconds before answering. "Yes. As a matter of fact, I did."

Laurel cast him a meaningful look. "I mean it, too."

The front entrance of the Department of Fish and Game was a large, airy room that looked more like a museum than the lobby of an office building. Scattered around on the walls and in glass display cases were stuffed and mounted examples of Alaskan wildlife. In addition to birds and small mammals such as squirrels, bats, and lemmings, there was a sleek wolf, a Dall sheep with distinctive spiraling horns, and a huge wooly musk ox. What was most impressive, however, was the tremendous grizzly. Standing on his hind legs, his gigantic paws poised menacingly, he was easily eight or nine feet high.

"Imagine meeting *this* guy in the woods," Laurel joked.

"Right now," Russ replied after swallowing hard, "I think I'd prefer wrestling with him to giving this presentation."

Laurel was about to say something consoling when a young woman in jeans and a faded blue-denim shirt came striding across the lobby toward them. She was wearing a welcoming smile.

"You must be Dr. Wells's protégés," she said. "We've been expecting you. I'm Dina Simons, a wildlife biologist."

"I'm Laurel Adams, and this is Russ Corcoran."

"Thanks for coming. We're all anxious to hear about your project."

"Uh, exactly how many people will be coming?" Russ asked anxiously.

"Only a dozen or so. Unfortunately, a lot of people weren't able to come in from the field this afternoon. But those of us who are coming promised to take notes and tell them all about it."

"Is Ben Seeger coming?" asked Laurel, lowering her backpack to the floor.

"He wouldn't miss it. He and Ethan have been friends for years. Ben's always interested in learning about what he and his students are up to. That's especially true this year, since Wolf Lake is in his territory.

"Why don't you come into my office?" Dina suggested. "You can leave your packs in there. Would you like a few minutes to look over your notes?"

A few minutes later, she led Laurel and Russ into a compact conference room. Seven or eight people sat around an oval-shaped table, waiting. Dina took a seat at its head.

"I'll wait until everyone gets here before making introductions. In the meantime," she added, gesturing toward the small table in the back corner of the room, "help yourselves to coffee."

A few more people straggled in. Most of them chatted with each other, although the man sitting next to Russ and Laurel asked them a few questions about their trip up from the Kenai Peninsula and their impressions of Anchorage.

Finally, a man sitting in back said, "Since we're all here, this might be a good time to get everyone's feedback on the proposal for the new budget. Anybody had a chance to look over that memo yet?"

As the others discussed department business, Laurel and Russ sat with their heads together, reading through their notes one last time and reviewing who'd be talking about which topic.

At ten minutes after three, Dina glanced at her watch and frowned. "Everyone's here except Ben. Where is he?"

"I saw him a few minutes ago," someone volunteered. "I'm pretty sure he's in the building."

"I hope he remembered to put today's meeting on his calendar."

"Do you want me to see if I can track Mr. Seeger down?" Laurel offered. "That way, the rest of you can finish your discussion."

"Would you?" Dina cast her a look of gratitude. "Start by checking his office. It's right down the hall."

Someone was already voicing a new opinion about the memo.

"I'll come with you," Russ whispered to Laurel. With a sheepish grin, he added, "My throat's kind of dry. I could use a drink of water."

"I think I noticed a drinking fountain around the corner," said Laurel.

She and Russ headed down the corridor. Sure enough, there was a water fountain at the end. Right before it was a door labeled "Ben Seeger. Enforcement Coordinator, Southcentral Alaska and Kodiak Island."

"I'll look in here," Laurel called to Russ.

She knocked on the open door, meanwhile glancing into the office. Finding it empty, she stepped inside. Mr. Seeger's calendar lay open on his desk. Curious about whether or not he'd remembered to make a note of today's meeting, she went over to the desk. Written underneath that day's date was "3:00—Dr. Wells." Yet as she stared at those simple words, she was suddenly overcome with a wave of dizziness.

That handwriting. She'd seen it before. And the letters had been written with the same distinctive pen. Fine lines in jet black ink. . . .

And then something else on the desk caught her eye. Half-hidden by a pile of pink telephone messages was a small notebook, about three by five inches. She hesitated, her mind racing. And then, without actually making a decision to do so, she picked it up.

Automatically the book fell open. Sticking out from the binding were the edges of a page that had been ripped out. The paper that remained formed a row of jagged, uneven triangles.

She recognized their pattern immediately.

"Everything okay in here?"

Laurel snapped her head up at the unexpected sound of Russ's voice. He was standing in the doorway, watching her with a concerned look on his face.

"Yes. I mean, no. I mean . . ." Laurel bit her lip. "I guess I'm not sure."

Coming into the room, he asked, "What's going on?"

She took a deep breath. "Either I'm running into one coincidence after another, or else I've found the guilty party."

"Guilty?" Russ frowned. "Of what? What are you talking about?"

She held up the small book she'd been examining. "Look familiar?"

"Sure. I've seen that kind of notebook before. A lot of people use them for fieldwork. They're called Write-in-the-Rain books, because they're made of special paper that keeps ink from being smeared when the weather's bad."

"Take a closer look, Russ." Laurel held it out for him to examine. "Now tell me if anything about this looks familiar."

As he took the book from her, his expression changed

quickly from one of confusion to one of horror. "Oh, no! Laurel, where did you find this?"

"Right here on Ben Seeger's desk. As a matter of fact, his name is written on the front cover. Not only is the handwriting familiar, it was also written with a Rapidograph."

Quickly Russ turned to the front of the book. After glancing at the name scrawled there, he looked up at Laurel.

Before either of them had a chance to speak, Dina came sailing in.

"I found him!" she declared brightly.

Ben Seeger was standing right behind her, a friendly smile on his face.

He was wearing a jacket made of red-plaid wool.

chapter
nineteen

"And in the live traps, we've caught red fox, raccoon, snowshoe hare, ground squirrel, red squirrel, red-backed vole, meadow vole, and meadow-jumping mouse." Mariah glanced up from the list she'd been reading as she lay stretched across the plaid couch. Her foot was elevated, balanced on a tower of pillows. "Is that it for the survey of mammals living around the lake?"

Cassie glanced up from the table, where she sat opposite Trip. "Don't forget the porcupine Laurel and I spotted the day we went to the supermarket," she added.

Thinking back to that day saddened her. She and Laurel, whom, at that point, she'd thought of as her best friend, had had such fun, jumping into the Jeep and heading into town. . . . Now, that day seemed light-years away. She glanced over at Trip, who was sitting with his hiking boots propped up on the edge of the table, his chair leaning back so far it threatened to topple over at any minute. She hoped to catch his eye. But he was absorbed in thumbing through the marble notebook in which he kept notes.

"I've spotted a few animals that we haven't gotten in the traps," Trip said. "I've been keeping a list." Having found the page he'd been looking for, he folded over his notebook. "Let's see. Coyote, northern flying squirrel . . . and here's the prizewinner, a marten."

"What's a marten?" Cassie asked.

"Martes americana," Trip replied. He sounded as if he were giving a lecture. "They're members of the weasel family, the *Mustelidae*. Martens are fairly small, about two feet long and low to the ground. They're bushy and brown, with rounded ears. But what's most distinctive about them is their face. They have pointed noses that make them look like foxes. A lot of native Alaskans go their whole lives without ever seeing one," he added boastfully. "Guess I've just got a particularly good eye."

"What else have you spotted, Oh Great One?" asked Mariah.

A knock outside the cabin door kept him from answering. Danny Torvold popped his head in, his bright eyes darting around the cabin.

"Is Russ here?" the boy asked hopefully.

"Nope," Trip replied, barely glancing over. "Sorry, kid."

"He's in Anchorage," Cassie explained. She went over to him, peering at the stack of wooden boxes he was holding. "Hey, what have you get there?"

"It's my insect collection. I wanted to show it to Russ."

"I'm sure he'll be disappointed that he missed it," Mariah commented dryly.

"When's he getting back?"

"Not until later tonight," said Cassie. "We'll be sure to tell him you stopped by." She stood by the door, expecting the little boy to leave.

Instead, he remained in the middle of the cabin, still clutching his collection tightly against his chest. He shifted his weight from one foot to the other. "So what are you guys doing?"

"Just trying to pull some of our notes together," Trip answered. "At least, we were before we were interrupted." His growing impatience was reflected in his tone.

"Maybe I could help." Danny set his collection down on the table. "I know this lake better than anybody."

"This is pretty technical stuff," Trip insisted. "What we do is a little more demanding than riding around in a canoe, looking at the pretty wildflowers."

"Oh, let him stay." Mariah leaned forward to fuss with the pillows under her foot. "Or are you afraid a nine-year-old kid's going to make you look bad?"

Trip cast her a dirty look, then turned back to his notes. "Okay. Where were we?"

"You were telling us how lucky you were to have spotted a wild marten."

"Oh, that's right. I *was* lucky. It's really hard to spot one—"

"What did he look like?" Danny asked enthusiastically.

"He was a perfect specimen," Trip replied. "Foxlike face, rounded ears. . . . What do you think he looked like? He looked like the martens I've seen in books."

Danny frowned. "Gee, Trip. I don't think that was a marten."

"What are you talking about?" Trip asked crossly. "Of course it was. Are you calling me a liar?"

"No, I'm just saying that it's really hard to spot one. I've only seen martens twice in my whole life."

"That's why it was so cool."

"Did it have a long bushy tail?"

"Huh?"

"Martens are different from other weasels because they have long, bushy tails."

Trip squirmed in his chair. "Uh, I don't remember seeing a long tail."

"So much for your *National Geographic* article," Mariah said, laughing. "Why don't you tell your fans how it feels to be outsmarted by a kid half your age?"

"I was just trying to be helpful," Danny protested. "I wasn't trying to show off!"

"We know that," Mariah said, still laughing. "It's Trip who's the show-off."

She stopped laughing as a peculiar sound suddenly cut through the cabin. It was low and irregular, like a growl.

Cassie looked up, blinking. "What was that?"

"Probably just the wind," said Trip.

"There's no wind tonight."

Nervously Cassie looked out the window. "Maybe it was a wild animal."

"Right." Trip made a face. "Something really scary . . . like a raccoon."

"Or a marten," Mariah muttered.

"You're probably right. It was probably just a—"

A loud crash right outside the cabin sent Danny rushing toward the doorway. He poked his head out through the thick curtain of mosquito netting. "It sounds like that raccoon's going through the garbage."

"There's no garbage out there," said Trip. "Just a pile of fish traps that Dr. Wells and I are going to clean when he gets back from Seward."

"That raccoon's going to be disappointed when he figures out there are no fish to go with the fish smell," Danny commented.

"Maybe we should close the door," Cassie suggested. "In case he comes running in here."

"Not likely," said Trip. "Besides, we'll suffocate. Leave it open."

"Maybe we can open the windows a little wider. The problem with them is that they're so darned small." Cassie went over to the nearest window, pretending she was checking it. In reality, she was peering out, anxious to see what was making that terrible racket.

Immediately her heart began to pound. Outside, in the dense brush, she saw something moving. A large shadowy shape, hovering just beyond the trees. . . .

"Something's out there!" she gasped. "Something *big!*"

Mariah rolled her eyes. "Maybe it's Jim Whitehorse, wanting to party."

Cassie remained glued to the window. "I don't think Jim Whitehorse would knock over fish traps."

"We should really get back to our list," Mariah said impatiently. "I don't know about the rest of you, but there are other things I'd like to do tonight besides play Animal Lotto—"

All of a sudden something crashed against the front of the cabin, so forcefully that the entire building shook. Mariah and Cassie exchanged terrified glances. Trip jerked his head up so abruptly that he toppled his chair over. He fell to the floor with a loud crash. Danny ran over to the window.

"What's going on?" Mariah shrieked. "An earthquake?"

"This is no earthquake," Danny replied, his voice a hoarse whisper. "It's a bear!"

"A bear!" Mariah could barely get the word out.

The pounding continued, each thrust of the bear's gigantic body growing stronger as with great determination he crashed against the cabin.

"Be quiet!" Trip instructed, scrambling to his feet,

not bothering to set the chair right. "Maybe he'll go away if he thinks there's no one here—"

"No," Danny insisted. "My dad always tells me to make a lot of noise. Yell, scream, hit pots and pans—"

"That's right," said Cassie, her voice shrill. "I remember that from the day we got here."

Mariah just stared at them from the couch, where she remained frozen to the spot. Cassie followed Danny as he raced toward the kitchen. She was gripped by a fear more terrible than any she'd ever known. It was almost impossible for her to breathe, and her heart was beating so furiously she felt nauseous. With trembling hands she took the frying pan and metal lid Danny gave her as he crouched in front of the cabinet.

"Here, Cassie," he commanded. "Bang these together. Trip, take these."

She felt as if she were in a nightmare, scarcely able to move. The muscles of her arms were paralyzed. But somehow, she found the strength to hit the lid against the back of the frying pan.

Trip was hitting a metal spoon against a saucepan, his face colorless. The clatter was deafening, but the bear continued pounding against the wall of the cabin.

"Close the front door, Mariah!" Cassie screeched.

"That won't help!" Trip shot back.

"Do *something*!" she cried. Tears were streaming down her face.

Moving like a robot, Mariah got up off the couch. Her eyes were wide with terror.

"Close the door!" Cassie yelled again. "Lock it!"

Mariah stood in the center of the cabin. She was only a few feet away from the door, yet she seemed unable to cross the short distance.

"Mariah!" Cassie's voice was shrill. "Close the door!"

Mariah let out a low, fearful moan.

In a small voice, Trip asked, "Can't we get somebody to help us? Isn't there a radio or something?"

"There's one at my house," Danny suggested. "Maybe I should run out and tell my mom and dad—"

"No!" Cassie instructed. "Stay right where you are, Danny! Don't you dare go outside. All we need is for the bear to see you. He'll be after you in no time."

"I can run fast," Danny insisted. "Maybe if I can outsmart him—"

"Danny, no!" Cassie cried.

Trip broke in, his voice shaky. "Why not? If the kid can get to a radio and get us some help—"

"You can't send him out there!" Cassie exclaimed.

"Well . . . what else are we going to do?" Trip demanded.

Mariah stood in the middle of the room, her entire body shaking. "Maybe—maybe he'll give up and just go away."

The four of them stood staring at the doorway. Through the mosquito netting, they could see the dark hulking frame of the bear as he banged against the building.

And then, as suddenly as the terrible noise had begun, it stopped.

For a few seconds there was silence. They all stood very still, barely breathing.

And then, in a flash, a monstrous paw came through the doorway, cutting the mosquito netting. A loud ripping sound accompanied the swift motion of the bear tearing with his sharp claws.

Cassie screamed. "He's coming in! He's after us!"

"Quick, up the ladder," Danny instructed. "We can get out through the window in the loft!"

Trip was already rushing toward the ladder. He ran

up it without once glancing back. The girls sent Danny up next. Mariah followed, letting out a yelp of pain as she put her weight on her sprained ankle. Cassie was right behind her.

"Come on, Mariah," she muttered. "Come *on!*"

"I don't know if I can!"

"You've *got* to!"

When the four had safely made it to the top, Cassie and Mariah pushed the ladder away. As it was falling to the floor, the bear crashed through, splintering the door frame with his massive body. The wooden ladder fell on top of him, and he let out a loud bellow.

"Okay, Trip. Open the window," Cassie instructed as calmly as she could. She kept her eyes glued to the bear. The grizzly was huge, his shoulders looming above the table, his body so long he nearly filled the front room. He moved his tremendous head from side to side as he surveyed the cabin, making an ominous growling sound. "Open the window!"

"It's stuck," Trip returned. "This screen is so rusty it won't budge!"

Cassie watched in horror as the bear moved about the cabin. Almost immediately he lumbered toward the kitchen. With one powerful paw he reached up and swatted at the collection of cans and boxes that lined the counter. They fell to the floor with a loud crash. He remained undaunted, sticking his nose into the mess as he searched for food.

"He's so big," Mariah whispered, her voice edged with panic.

"Please, Trip. Get that window open!" Cassie begged.

"It's stuck. I can't—"

"Trip, *please!*"

"Got it!" he finally shouted.

The sound of his voice caused the bear to look up at the loft. Standing frozen to the spot, he stared blankly at the four people hovering high above him. Slowly Cassie backed away from the edge, moving closer to the window.

"We've got to get out—*now!*" she commanded.

Glancing over her shoulder, she saw that Trip was already doing just that. He climbed out the window, disappearing from sight as he dropped to the ground.

"I can't do it!" Mariah screamed. "My ankle hurts too much!"

"You have no choice," Cassie insisted. "Jump, Mariah!"

"But what if he follows us outside?" Mariah grabbed hold of Cassie's arm, clutching it so tightly it hurt. The two stood frozen to the spot, their eyes following the bear. He already seemed to have lost interest in them, instead turning his attention back to the food piled up on the floor.

"Mariah's right," Danny said in a thin voice. "Maybe we're better off staying up here."

Cassie looked first at the bear, then at the open window. She hesitated, not knowing what to do. It was so hard to think clearly when her mind was clouded by such a deep, sickening fear. The one thing she was sure about was that she had to make a decision fast—and that making the right choice could well determine whether or not she'd survive.

Laurel and Russ were silent as they drove down the bumpy dirt road toward the cabin. It had been a long, tiring day. Having discovered that Ben Seeger was behind the bear poachings had been devastating. Yet, thinking about what still lay ahead—having to tell Dr. Wells the truth about his longtime friend and turning him in to the proper authorities—was almost as over-whelming.

"I wonder if Dr. Wells will be back from town yet," Laurel mused as the Jeep rounded the last bend in the dirt road and the roof of the cabin came into sight. "In a way, I hope he won't be. I'm not exactly looking for-ward to telling him."

"We have to," Russ said gently. "It's the only way."

"I know." Laurel bit her lip. Not only was she upset over how wrong she'd been about the conservation of-ficer, it was also hard for her to accept the fact that someone in authority, whose job it was to *protect*, could actually be guilty of committing the very crimes he was supposed to be preventing. Her heart was heavy from the lesson she'd learned: things weren't always as they seemed ... or as they should be.

She'd been ruminating during the entire ride back from Anchorage. Yet as the cabin came into view, all thoughts about Ben Seeger and the bear poaching in-stantly vanished. Automatically she jammed on the brakes.

Laurel could scarely believe what she was seeing: Trip leaping out of the loft window, falling to the ground with a thud. She watched in astonishment as a look of pain crossed his face, then faded quickly to one of absolute terror.

From inside the cabin came a great racket. Thumps and crashes and the sound of glass breaking exploded through the walls. It almost sounded as if dishes and cans and jars were being thrown from the kitchen shelves. What was even more alarming was the low, un-even growling sound that accompanied it.

"What's happening?" Laurel demanded, bewildered.

Trip was already rushing toward the car, moving so quickly over the rough terrain that he stumbled twice.

"Bear!" he gasped, his eyes wild. "There's a bear in the cabin!"

"A bear?" Laurel repeated, gripping the steering wheel. "Where are the others?"

"Inside." He was gasping for breath.

Russ leaped out of the passenger side. "Trip, is the pepper spray still on the shelf by the front door?"

"What?" Trip stared at him blankly.

"The pepper spray, Trip. Has anyone moved it?"

"I-I don't know. I can't think—"

Russ turned to Laurel, sitting paralyzed in the driver's seat. "Laurel, I'll get the others out. Help them into the Jeep. Once everyone's inside, drive away from here as fast as you can."

Terror was rising up inside her. "What are you going to do?"

"I'll try to ward off the bear before he destroys the cabin, our notes, our equipment—" Russ was already darting toward the cabin.

"You're not going in there alone!"

"Just do it!" He crossed the few yards that separated the Jeep from the cabin in a few long strides, yelling, "Cassie? Mariah? Get out! Get in the car!"

Only a few seconds passed before Danny Torvold's head emerged from the loft window. He hesitated briefly, then jumped out. He fell to the soft ground, then scrambled to his feet and raced toward the car.

Cassie came next, moving more slowly and more awkwardly than the little boy. Her face was red, and she grimaced when she hit the ground. Instead of running toward the car, she turned her face up to the window, holding out her arms.

"Okay, Mariah. You can do it. Jump toward me, and I'll break your fall."

"But my ankle!" Mariah cried.

"Don't worry about your ankle. Try landing on your other foot. You've got to get out of there!"

Mariah climbed out slowly, her face twisted with pain. When she finally leapt out of the window, she fell against Cassie. Both of them let out yelps as they tumbled over. Mariah's leg was bleeding as she stood up, and she kicked away the sharp branch that had scraped her. But at least she was out of the cabin. Cassie grabbed her around the waist and helped her toward the Jeep.

Cassie and Mariah finally made it inside the car. Mariah climbed in front and Cassie got in back with Trip and Danny. But they weren't all out of danger—at least, not yet. Laurel sat gripping the steering wheel as she watched the cabin anxiously.

"What are you waiting for?" Trip asked, his voice edged with hysteria. "Let's get out of here!"

"Trip, Russ is in there!" Cassie reminded him.

"Get us out of here!" Trip demanded.

"We have to wait for Russ," Laurel insisted. She kept her eyes fixed on the cabin. From inside she could hear the bear's growls.

And then, suddenly, he let out a loud bellow. It cut through the forest like a gunshot. The earth seemed to tremble as the giant animal came crashing out of the cabin. All five of them watched as the bear took off, running into the forest, the dense growth of trees finally swallowing him up.

Laurel's hands were clutched against her chest as she struggled to catch her breath. "Is everybody all right?"

"I think so," Cassie assured her, panting.

"At least we are now," Mariah added. "Laurel, if you and Russ hadn't shown up when you did, I don't know what would have happened to us."

"Thanks, Laurel," Cassie said. "You sure have good timing."

Laurel peered at Trip through the rearview mirror. He was sitting slumped over in the backseat, his arms folded protectively around himself, his blue eyes wide. His face was completely drained of blood, his expression one of shock. Her first impression could well have been that he was just kidding around. But she could see that his terror was real.

"It's okay now, Trip," Laurel said soothingly, turning around to look at him over her shoulder. "You're safe."

"The bear's gone," Danny assured him. "With that pepper spray in his eyes, he won't bother us again for a long time."

Russ came out of the cabin then, his face red, his straight brown hair falling into his eyes. He walked with his shoulders slumped, as if he were completely drained.

"Is he gone?" he demanded, blinking hard as he looked around. "I-I couldn't see out the window that well."

"Yes, he's gone," said Laurel. "We saw him run into the woods."

Now that Russ was close, Laurel could see his eyes were tearing from the pepper spray. "He was a big one." His voice was shaky. "A full-grown male. I'd put him at well over a thousand pounds—"

"Get in the car," Laurel suggested gently. "Let's get out of here."

Russ glanced back at the cabin. "We might as well. That pepper spray's so potent it'll be some time before we can go back into the cabin again." He shook his head. "I'm anxious to see how bad the damage is. I'm afraid that bear really did a number on the place."

"The only thing that matters," said Laurel, "is that we're all safe."

It sounded like such a simple, obvious thing to say. Yet never before had those words seemed so true.

chapter
twenty

"Wow." Dr. Wells shook his head slowly, glancing up from the stack of notes he was putting back in order. "The five of you certainly had a harrowing experience."

"You mean the six of us," Russ corrected him. Sweeping up the refuse left behind by the bear, he paused. "Don't forget Danny."

Laurel nodded in agreement. "I'm sure last night was a night he'll remember for the rest of his life."

It was early the next day. After spending a restless night crowded into the Torvolds' cabin, curled up on the floor with sleeping bags and blankets, the group had come back to their own cabin. Dr. Wells ventured inside first, wanting to see if the air had been sufficiently cleared of the pepper spray for them to enter. Once he'd decided it was safe, the others had gone in, curious to see just how much damage the bear had done.

For two hours they'd toiled. Cleaning up the kitchen turned out to be the most tedious job. Laurel and the others labored over the broken jars of honey and maple syrup that had mixed with the mounds of cereal and rolled oats spilled on the floor. Not quite as messy, but at least as frustrating, was putting their papers back in order. The bear had knocked over the table, sending files and neat stacks of notes sprawling across the floor in a state of complete disarray.

But that had been just the beginning of the destruction wreaked by the bear. Trip and Cassie took down the shredded mosquito netting that had once lined the doorway and would now have to be replaced. Russ and Laurel scraped muddy paw prints off the front porch and the floors. As for the long, deep claw marks that marred the exterior of the building, as well as the floor and the wooden table, they could not be cleared away as easily. That was also true of the torn couch. A single swipe of the giant beast's claw had shredded the seat cushion from one end to the other. Foam-rubber stuffing was already spilling out.

Finally, Cassie and Trip volunteered to carry out the bags containing the broken bottles, spilled food, and ripped netting. Mariah retired to her room to rest her aching foot.

"Well," said Laurel, standing in the middle of the living area with her hands on her hips, "maybe the cabin suffered a few scars. But at least none of us did."

Dr. Wells nodded. "Thank goodness for that."

The loud roar of an engine, moving closer and closer, came as a surprise, breaking into the otherwise peaceful silence that surrounded the cabin. Laurel glanced out the doorway and saw a floatplane hovering above Wolf Lake. Printed on the side were the words "Alaska Department of Fish and Game."

Dr. Wells joined her at the door as she watched the plane dip lower and lower, the massive balloonlike pontoons on either side allowing it to land on the surface of the water.

"That's Ben Seeger for you," said Dr. Wells, chuckling. "John Torvold radioed him first thing this morning, and he's already on the scene."

Laurel's reaction to the arrival of the seaplane was quite different. An uncomfortable knot had already formed in her stomach. With all the excitement of the bear's attack on the cabin, she'd completely forgotten about the discovery she and Russ had made in Anchorage the day before. Now, she was reminded of the difficult task before her.

"Dr. Wells," she said nervously, checking over her shoulder to make sure the others were out of earshot, "there's something Russ and I have to talk to you about. In private."

"Can't it wait? I'm sure Ben's going to want you to fill him in on what happened last night. No doubt there'll be a written report to file—"

"It's pretty important." Laurel drew in her breath sharply. "Dr. Wells, I think Russ and I have figured out who's responsible for the bear poachings around Wolf Lake. Yesterday, when we were at the Department of Fish and Game—"

"I'm anxious to hear what you have to say, Laurel, but I'm afraid we'll have to hold off until later," Dr. Wells insisted. "Right now, I'd better see if Ben needs any help." He hurried down the path to greet his friend, leaving Laurel standing in the doorway.

A few minutes later he and Ben Seeger were making their way up the path from the lake toward the cabin. "Sounds like you had some trouble last night," Laurel heard Ben say as the two men drew near.

"That's an understatement," Dr. Wells replied.

"Torvold assured me that everybody was okay," Ben said, climbing the steps to the cabin. "It sounds like your people all behaved like heroes. Danny, too."

"Everyone's fine," Dr. Wells assured him as he went into the cabin, with Ben and Laurel right behind him. "A little shaken up, of course. But it could have been a lot worse. And as you can see, after a morning of hard work, we've got things pretty much back in order."

Ben cast Laurel a friendly smile. "It looks like you put in a hard morning's work." Glancing around, he commented, "But it does look like you'll need a new couch."

Dr. Wells grinned. "That old thing was on its last legs anyway."

"Hello, Russ," Ben said, nodding toward the boy standing in the kitchen, wiping off the kitchen counter.

"Hi, Mr. Seeger."

Laurel and Russ exchanged meaningful glances. Ben didn't seem to notice.

"I'm hoping the witnesses will give me as much detail about what happened as they can," he said. "I'll need to file a report with the Department."

"I'm sure that won't be a problem. In the meantime," said Dr. Wells, "there's something else brewing that I think you'll be interested in. Laurel seems to think she's uncovered the mystery behind the bear poachings."

Ben Seeger's friendly smile faded. "What are you talking about?"

"I'm not sure. What is it you wanted to tell me, Laurel? This is as good a time as any, since this is Ben's area of responsibility."

This time the look Laurel cast Russ was one of alarm.

"Do you want me to start, Laurel?" he asked softly.

"No. I. . . ." She swallowed hard. "Dr. Wells, Russ and I think Mr. Seeger might know more about the bear poachings than we thought."

Dr. Wells frowned. "I'm afraid I don't understand."

"Maybe you'd better show Dr. Wells the note, Laurel," Russ suggested.

"I've got it right here." Laurel drew the warning letter out of her backpack and showed it to Dr. Wells. "Maybe we should have shown it to you sooner, but we wanted to wait until we figured out who sent it. Look at the jagged edge—and the strange paper it's written on."

Dr. Wells held the note in his hand, peering at it. "This is a page out of a Write-in-the-Rain pad, isn't it?"

"Exactly." Biting her lip, she said, "Yesterday, when Russ and I were in Anchorage, I stumbled across Mr. Seeger's pad. I couldn't help noticing that there was a page ripped out . . . a page with an edge that looked very much like this one."

Ben Seeger's eyes had narrowed. "What are you implying?"

Dr. Wells looked puzzled. "You must have brought along your Write-in-the-Rain book, Ben, didn't you?"

Ben kept his cold gaze on Laurel a little longer before turning his attention to Dr. Wells. "To tell you the truth, I'm not sure I have it today."

"Why don't you check your backpack?" Dr. Wells suggested. "Maybe it will help get this settled once and for all."

"Well, I—" He hesitated, looking from Dr. Wells to Russ and then back to Laurel. With a loud sigh, he dropped his pack on the wooden floor and began rifling through it. "Here it is. Now if you'd just tell me what this is all about—"

"May I see it?" Laurel took the book from him. She opened it, expecting to see the same jagged edge she'd stumbled upon yesterday. Yet much to her amazement, it was gone. The only thing the least bit unusual about the book was a single even edge, about a half-inch wide, that stuck out near the binding. It was clear that a page had been ripped out—but whatever telltale signs had been left behind had been trimmed with a razor.

"But—but I thought . . . yesterday, in your office. . . ." Desperately Laurel looked at Russ. He was wearing a look of confusion that echoed what she was feeling.

Dr. Wells was frowning. "Laurel, Russ, I think you need to go back to the beginning and tell me what this is all about."

She could feel her face turning red. "There has to be some explanation."

"There is," a male voice suddenly boomed. "A perfectly good explanation."

She whirled around. Looming in the doorway was Jim Whitehorse. In his hand was a large manila envelope.

"Whitehorse!" Ben Seeger said. "How long have you been standing there?"

"Long enough to hear what these two had to say. And to realize that it's time for my long silence to end."

"Keep out of this, Whitehorse," Ben said. "None of this is your concern!"

"As a matter of fact, it's very much my concern." Jim Whitehorse's cold gaze rested on Ben for a long time before he turned his attention to the others. "Dr. Wells, what Laurel and Russ thought they figured out yesterday happens to be one hundred percent true. Maybe they can't prove it . . . but I can."

Dr. Wells looked astonished. "Surely you're not saying you think Ben is responsible for the bear poachings!"

"I'm afraid our state official here has discovered there's more money to be made by breaking the laws then by upholding them."

The tall man spoke in a low, even voice. "Over the past six or eight months, Ben has been regularly leading visitors to the Kenai out on adventurous expeditions. He guarantees them a front-row seat in a bear-hunting expedition—one that just happens to be illegal. He gets the opportunity to make a great deal of money. The tourists, meanwhile, get the thrill of watching an 'expert'—an expert who deftly chases and herds bears. They even get to bring home a claw as a souvenir. It makes a lovely paperweight, a real conversation piece. Of course, some people prefer to wear them around their necks, on a chain. Kind of like a trophy.

"Yes, Mr. Seeger here had a nice little sideline going. And carrying it off was simple. He had access to the planes, no one looking over his shoulder. . . . As for the tourists, they had a grand time. There was only one rule: no photographs. Fortunately, that rule doesn't apply to those of us who only hunt bears according to the rules."

Ben Seeger looked as if he were going to burst. "Why, you. . . . Lies! These are all lies, I tell you!"

Dr. Wells held up his hand for silence. "Let him speak."

Jim Whitehorse glared at Ben before going on. "Three or four months ago, when I first discovered that Ben was padding his own pockets by taking tourists on these little hunting trips, I confronted him. He tried to blackmail me, saying that if I didn't keep my mouth shut, he'd find a way to pin the poachings on me.

"A threat like that was something to think about. After all, I don't have the political connections this man has. I'm not pals with the local police, the way he is. If it ever came down to my word against his, there'd be no contest."

Jim shook his head slowly. "To tell you the truth, I've been wrestling with this problem for a long time. I'm a man who likes to keep to himself. I'm happy having as little to do with the outside world—especially the government—as possible.

"But I can't keep silent any longer. I've been having

a hard enough time living with myself. I find my happiness living off this land, just like the bears and the other animals around Wolf Lake. If they aren't safe here, then neither am I."

"So you were right," Dr. Wells said to Laurel and Russ. "This little investigation of yours really did lead you to the guilty party."

Jim nodded in their direction. "These two did a fine job. In fact, knowing that these kids were willing to invest their time and energy trying to get to the bottom of this dirty little mystery was a big factor in helping me decide to come forward with the truth. Frankly, I was kind of worried about what might happen to them. Ben knew they were sniffing around, trying to come up with some answers. He saw them that day they came to my cabin. He was there, looking for me. He'd come around every now and then to make sure I wasn't getting any funny ideas. I guess that's the day he left them that note."

"Yes," said Laurel, nodding. "That's exactly when we found it."

Jim Whitehorse held out the envelope. "These photographs are all you'll need. Just hand them over to the authorities; they'll know what to do."

Before pressing the envelope into Dr. Wells's hand, he added, "I know Ben's a friend of yours. I'm sure you must feel torn over this. But I hope that, in the end, you'll do what's right."

Slowly Dr. Wells opened the envelope. His expression grew stricken as he looked through the black-and-white photographs. The one that Laurel glanced at was a picture of two planes, flying low to the ground. Not far below them was a bear. A man was leaning out of one of the planes with a hunting rifle pointed at the bear. And the identity of the man was unmistakable.

He slid the photos back into the envelope, then cast a questioning look at his old friend. Ben Seeger, in turn, was unable to meet his gaze.

"Yes," Dr. Wells said simply. "I have no choice but to do what's right."

He glanced first at Laurel, then at Russ. He said nothing, but his eyes were filled with sadness.

The next morning, an air of lethargy hung about the cabin. Dr. Wells left the lake early, not even taking the time for breakfast. Mariah sat on the front porch, distractedly massaging her sore ankle as she watched him climb into the Jeep. She was struck by the slump of his shoulders and his look of grim determination as he headed into Anchorage to do a job he was hardly looking forward to, yet knew had to be done.

She gradually became aware that she wasn't the only one watching his departure. Glancing over her shoulder, she saw that Laurel stood right behind her. She was leaning in the doorway and shielding her eyes against the sun, pale and round as it hovered low in the gray-blue sky.

"You know," Laurel mused, "when I opened that notebook and saw that the jagged edge was gone, I was almost relieved. My first thought was that I'd been wrong, that Mr. Seeger really didn't have anything to do with the bear poachings."

"Jim Whitehorse took care of any doubts you may have had," said Mariah. "Those photographs of his made it clear that Seeger was taking would-be hunters for joyrides. I can't believe we all misjudged him so badly. I know Trip and the others feel just as betrayed as I do—not to mention Dr. Wells.

"I can't stop thinking about those poor bears! Can

you imagine how terrified they must have been, having not one but two planes hunt them down?"

"I still can't quite believe it." Shaking her head slowly, Laurel came over to the edge of the porch and sat down next to Mariah. "This whole thing has been like a dream. Or maybe I should say a nightmare. All of it seems so unreal: finding the dead bears, launching our own small-time investigation, finding that note. . . ."

She fell silent, picking up a twig and drawing designs in the dirt below the porch. "You know, Mariah," she said slowly, "I have a confession to make." She kept her eyes down as she said, "For a while, I suspected that you were the one who sent me that note."

"Me?" Mariah repeated, incredulous. "How on earth did you ever come up with that conclusion?"

"Your pen. The note Ben Seeger left for me to find had been written with a Rapidograph. Right after you hurt your ankle, when I was getting paper out of your backpack, I found yours."

"It's true that I happen to own a Rapidograph. But so do a few million other people. That still doesn't explain why I'd go around leaving weird notes for you to find."

Laurel shrugged. "I thought you were jealous."

"Well, of all the. . . ." Mariah let her voice trail off. "You're right, Laurel. I was jealous of you."

For a moment Laurel was silent, trying to digest the full meaning of her confession. "I guess that explains a lot. About why you and I have never been able to be friends, I mean." Glancing over shyly, she asked, "But why, Mariah? Why would someone like you ever be jealous of me? You're smart, you're accomplished, you're a whiz at science—"

"Dr. Ames's research project, for one thing. I wanted to be picked for that so badly." With a cold laugh, she added, "Mainly because I figured it'd look good on my transcript when I applied to medical schools."

Laurel nodded. "It probably would have. But you've just finished your freshman year. You've still got lots of time for special projects that'll help your applications stand out."

"Funny thing about that." Mariah swept away a strand of long dark hair that had fallen into her eyes and gazed off into the distance. "Last night, when I was up in the loft and that bear was looking right at me, for the first time in my life I really understood that we're all on this planet for a limited time. At our age, it's hard to comprehend. But when a thousand pound monster's staring at you from less than ten feet away, that fact suddenly seems incredibly real.

"I've always heard that a person's whole life flashes before her eyes just before she dies. Yet it wasn't the part of my life that's behind me that I saw, it was the part that's still ahead of me. And standing up there in the loft, wondering if I was going to get out of there alive or not, I suddenly realized something."

"What?" asked Laurel.

"That I don't want to spend my life being a doctor. And that the only reason I've been telling myself I wanted to go to medical school is because it's what my father and both my brothers did. Somewhere along the line, I managed to talk myself into believing it's what my mother would have wanted me to do, too."

Tears were welling up in her eyes. Yet instead of blinking them away, embarrassed over being caught crying, she let them stream down her cheeks. "I never really had a chance to get to know my mother. Of course, I have memories of her from when I was a little girl. But she died when I was only ten years old."

Glancing at Laurel, she added, "You didn't know that, did you?"

"No."

"How could you? I never told you. I never told anyone. Not about my mother—or very much else about myself, either. I was trying to protect myself. I figured if people didn't know much about me, they wouldn't be able to hurt me." She bit her lip. "But do you know what? They didn't have to. I've been doing a good enough job of hurting myself.

"My love of science is sincere, Laurel. But I think that what I need to do is step back and decide what I really want to do." Gesturing toward the magnificent woods stretching out before them, she added, "Who knows? Maybe I'll even end up coming back to Alaska, working as a field biologist."

"That'd be great," said Laurel. "But I have one piece of advice."

"What's that?"

"Leave your hair dryer home."

The joyful laughter of two young women cut through the stillness of the forest, a sound as sweet as the chirping of the birds and the rustling of the leaves.

Cassie stood on the edge of the clearing, watching Russ untie a row of knots that had formed in the strings of the fish traps with strong, confident hands. The early morning sun was shining through the trees at a low angle, lighting up his face. On it she could see an expression of complete contentment.

"Russ?" she said softly, taking a step toward him.

He turned, surprised. "Oh, hi, Cassie. I didn't know you were out here."

"I-I wanted to get you alone so I could say thank you."

Russ laughed, waving his hand in the air dismissively. "Oh, it was nothing. Taking out knots, fending off bears . . . as far as I'm concerned, it's all in a day's work."

She laughed, then quickly grew serious once again. "I think you were incredibly brave."

"Maybe if I'd had the time to stop and think about what I was doing, I wouldn't have done it. But at the time it just seemed like the thing to do."

"Very few people would have had the courage to go into the cabin after a bear. Especially armed with nothing more than a spray can!"

Russ shrugged. "I've fought off wild animals before." With a self-conscious grin, he added, "Of course, never anything bigger than a crazed squirrel."

He pushed aside the dark bangs that had fallen into his eyes. "You were pretty brave, too. Mariah and Danny both claim that if it hadn't been for your level-headedness, they never would have got out of there alive."

She could feel her cheeks turning pink. "I wouldn't go that far."

"It sounds like you were pretty amazing." Russ's voice had grown softer. "You know, Cassie," he went on, "I've been thinking about what I said to you. Remember, about how you're a really special girl and all?"

Cassie nodded. By now, she was certain her cheeks had to be a bright shade of scarlet.

"Believe it or not, not long ago somebody actually gave me almost the exact same speech. And hearing it from the other side made me realize two things. One is that that person was probably right. Even though the words can easily come out sounding like whoever's saying them is just trying to make you feel better, they really are true. About me . . . and about you.

"The other thing is that you really are special, Cassie." Russ hesitated a few seconds, then reached over and gently took Cassie's hand in his. "So special, in fact, that lately I've found myself wondering if maybe you and I could try to get to know each other better."

He was looking at her with a strange intensity. Cassie could feel her heartbeat quicken. He took a step closer, his brown eyes fixed on hers. She realized for the first time that that was what she wanted, too. Slowly, everything else was slipping away: the field stretching ahead of her, the forest all around, even the endless gray-blue sky, reaching up forever. Knowing that kissing Russ was going to be one of the most special moments of her life, she raised her face to his.

"Cassie?" Laurel asked, cocking her head to one side. "Are you all right?"

As she'd wandered into the girls' bedroom in the cabin, Cassie looked as if she were about to burst. Her cheeks were flushed, her green eyes were shining, and there was a distinctive lilt to her step.

"As a matter of fact," she replied, wearing a huge grin, "I've never felt better in my life!"

Laurel frowned. "This doesn't have anything to do with Trip, does it?"

"Trip? *Trip?* Do me a favor. Please don't ever mention that name to me again!"

Laurel laughed. "Whoa. Let's go back. I think I missed something here."

Cassie sat down on the edge of her bed. "You were absolutely right about Trip. He really is a despicable jerk."

"That's funny. After what happened yesterday, I'd actually started to feel sorry for him."

"*Sorry* for him? The boy's an absolute turkey! You

should have seen the way he acted when that bear showed up. Oh, sure, I could forgive him for the way he totally fell apart. He couldn't help that. But he became a madman! He raced ahead of the rest of us when we were trying to get out of the cabin. He even cut ahead of Danny! What's even worse, though, is that he wanted to send the poor kid outside to get help while *he* stayed safe and sound in the cabin!"

She shook her head in disgust. "How could I ever have been so wrong about someone?"

"At least you found out what Trip Raynor's really like."

"Too bad it took a bear attack to shake me out of my stupor."

"So if it isn't Trip who's responsible for that silly grin you were wearing when you came in here, who is?"

Cassie smiled shyly. "Russ."

"Russ!" Laurel could hardly believe her ears. And yet, now that she thought about it, it all made sense. Perfect sense. And she couldn't have been more pleased.

"Cassie, that's wonderful! I had no idea—"

"Neither did I. At least, not until a few minutes ago. But you know, Russ is an unusual guy. I think he's really special."

Laurel smiled. "I do, too. And I'm really happy for you."

"Which brings me to the apology I've owed you for a long time now. Laurel, I'm really sorry about how I've been treating you. Ever since we got up here, I've acted like such a baby!"

"No, you haven't," Laurel replied. "You acted like someone in the throes of her first serious crush." She looked at Cassie earnestly. "At least you've got things in better perspective now."

"I'll say," Cassie agreed. A slow smile crept across her face. "Of course, I don't expect to eat or sleep for the rest of my life. . . ."

"You know, Russ had an effect on me, too." Laurel held up the pad of paper that had been resting in her lap. "When you came in, I was writing a letter to my mother. At first, I figured I'd keep quiet about the fact that last night Papa Bear came to visit the cabin in which her little girl is living. But then I remembered something Russ told me a few weeks ago."

"What did he say?" Cassie asked, blinking.

"He said that because he'd grown up on a preserve, pretty much cut off from the rest of the world, he'd always been forced to look inside himself for answers. He convinced me that that's where the answers lie—not in other people's expectations."

With a shrug, she added, "He made me realize that I'm just going to have to keep on being the person I am, hoping that sooner or later my mother will come to accept it."

"Maybe some of that will rub off on me," Cassie said, smiling wistfully. "Maybe one of these days I'll leave Mountainville behind, run off to art school, spend all my waking hours drawing and painting and leading the wild, romantic life of an artist. . . ."

"Who knows?" Laurel replied seriously. "Maybe you will."

Just then, Mariah popped her head in. "What do you think this is, summer camp? We've got work to do!"

Cassie groaned. "You mean we don't get a day off to recover from a bear attack?"

"Are you kidding?" Mariah countered. "Dr. Wells expects us to pick up right where we left off. We've got traps to set, plants to press, butterflies to collect—"

Cassie sighed. "It never ends, does it?"

"No," said Laurel. "There's always more to do. More to learn. And more to experience." Tossing aside her pad of paper, she jumped off the bed. "Come on, you two. Let's hit the canoes!"

She strode out of the cabin, onto the porch. She paused there for just a moment, appreciating the warm sunlight on her face, the rich fragrance of the forest, the sweet sound of the birds. And then, with her chin held high and a satisfied smile on her face, she headed down the path, toward the edge of the lake.